Janet
Enjoy!
[signature]

GIFT OF DREAMS

GIFT OF DREAMS
BLACK FALLS NOVEL

KELLY ROSE SACCONE

iUniverse

GIFT OF DREAMS
BOOK 1

Copyright © 2018 Kelly Rose Saccone.

All rights reserved. No part of this book may be used or reproduced by any means, graphic, electronic, or mechanical, including photocopying, recording, taping or by any information storage retrieval system without the written permission of the author except in the case of brief quotations embodied in critical articles and reviews.

This is a work of fiction. All of the characters, names, incidents, organizations, and dialogue in this novel are either the products of the author's imagination or are used fictitiously.

iUniverse books may be ordered through booksellers or by contacting:

iUniverse
1663 Liberty Drive
Bloomington, IN 47403
www.iuniverse.com
1-800-Authors (1-800-288-4677)

Because of the dynamic nature of the Internet, any web addresses or links contained in this book may have changed since publication and may no longer be valid. The views expressed in this work are solely those of the author and do not necessarily reflect the views of the publisher, and the publisher hereby disclaims any responsibility for them.

Any people depicted in stock imagery provided by Getty Images are models, and such images are being used for illustrative purposes only.
Certain stock imagery © Getty Images.

ISBN: 978-1-4917-9887-4 (sc)
ISBN: 978-1-4917-9886-7 (e)

Library of Congress Control Number: 2018900171

Print information available on the last page.

iUniverse rev. date: 02/08/2018

Contents

Chapter	1	1
Chapter	2	19
Chapter	3	29
Chapter	4	33
Chapter	5	35
Chapter	6	41
Chapter	7	49
Chapter	8	53
Chapter	9	63
Chapter	10	77
Chapter	11	91
Chapter	12	109
Chapter	13	127
Chapter	14	145
Chapter	15	167
Chapter	16	181
Chapter	17	187
Chapter	18	207
Chapter	19	231

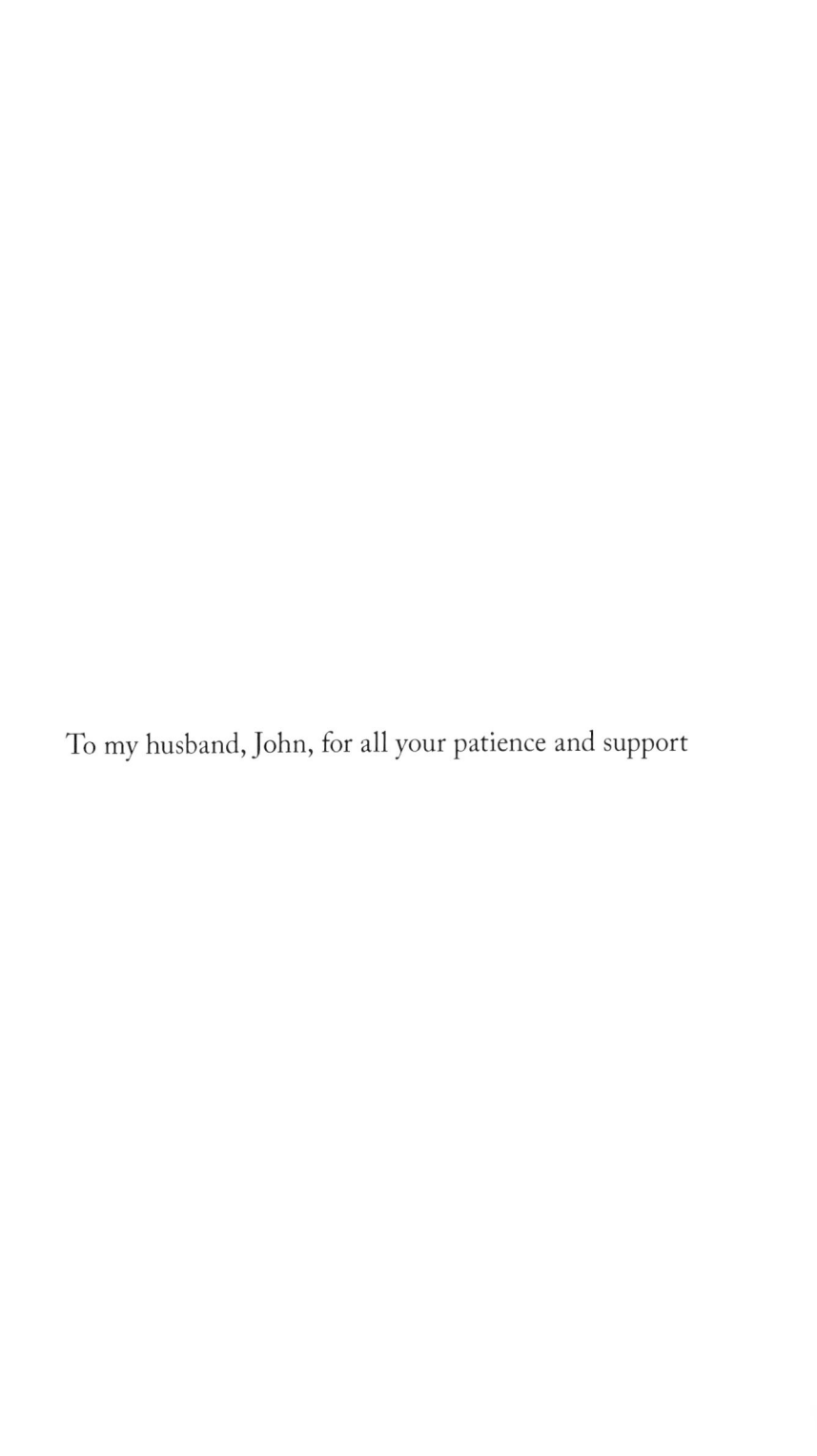

To my husband, John, for all your patience and support

Acknowledgments

I wish to acknowledge all the help provided by John Saccone, Pauline Hebeler, Margielou Peters, Nadine Bidwell, Sally Banyon, and Aaron Mullin, who read my story during its many metamorphoses and gave insight into how bad guys really talk.

1

Iris woke up and moaned. Her stomach heaved, making her gag on bile. She rubbed her belly and curled her body into a tight ball.

"Mommy," she whimpered.

❧

Rafe Wolf held his sister Gabby Richards in his arms. Her daughter Iris had been kidnapped. They were within the twenty-four-hour mark, but the clock was ticking.

Gabby sobbed. "She's dead, isn't she?"

Rafe looked down at his sister. His warm amber-brown eyes filled with concern as he stroked her hair. "Honey, you can't think like that. Sheriff Johnson wants me to meet some woman he thinks can help us find Iris. Let's give her a chance." Rafe wiped the tears from his sister's face.

Gabby pushed herself out of Rafe's arms and stomped

over to the kitchen, pulling out ingredients, nearly cracking the eggs she pulled from the refrigerator. Rafe watched, bemused, as cabinet doors slammed and the refrigerator door was opened and then slammed shut again. She pulled out a big bowl and smashed it down on the counter. She turned toward the stove and stared at it like it was an alien life-form. Her body shook. Gabby shook her head and then turned on the oven.

"Hon, are you going to be okay here while I go to the sheriff's office? Deputy Jones will stay here with you." Rafe lifted his hands in a helpless gesture.

Gabby dumped ingredients into the bowl. She pulled out a wooden spoon from a drawer and started to mix the ingredients. Flour flew out of the bowl. Rafe walked behind Gabby and grabbed her hands.

Gabby's shoulders tensed. "I don't understand any of this, Rafe. Who could have taken my baby? My beautiful little girl. One moment we're looking at books. Then the next she's gone. She's just gone." Gabby's body trembled.

Rafe tried to turn Gabby around to face him, but she stubbornly clung to the counter, staring at the ingredients in the bowl. "What if she's hurt? What …" Her head hung as tears slid down her face.

Suddenly she stood up straight, grabbed the spoon again, and banged it against the counter. "Goddamn it, who the fuck took my kid! What is happening to her?" Her shoulders slumped. I …" She turned to her brother. "What if she's dead? What will I do then?"

Rafe gathered Gabby into his arms and hugged her tightly to him, knowing he could not say anything to give her comfort. "Gabby, please, you need to calm down in case the kidnappers call. In case John calls with news."

Rafe looked around the kitchen. A butcher-block island dominated the room. A two-oven stove and double-door refrigerator were directly behind the island. It was a perfect kitchen for a serious chef.

Rafe stood back a little and brushed the hair off Gabby's face as he remembered his sister as a little girl, always baking something, especially when she was upset. He hid his smile as he recalled how many toy oven sets she went through as a child. Now she baked the desserts at her husband John's restaurant.

"Sweetheart, I really need to meet with Sheriff Johnson and this woman. John is with the FBI, and you need to be here in case the kidnappers call," Rafe said again. He slowly turned Gabby back toward the counter, picked up the spoon, and put it in her hand. "Why don't you finish what you started to make?" Rafe looked into the bowl of ingredients. "Cookies, is it? I know this is hard for you, and I want to stay with you. But I'll be back before you know it. I'm sure Deputy Jones would enjoy a cookie. Do you think you'll be okay while I'm gone?" Rafe asked in a calm voice.

Gabby shuddered and plucked at the sleeve of her oversize blue sweater. She swore and gripped the spoon tighter. Then she started mixing the batter. "Fine, Rafe. Fine. I'll bake some damn cookies." Gabby put the spoon down and searched for a tissue. She tore off a paper towel and blew her nose. "When do you meet with the sheriff and this woman?"

Rafe looked at his watch. "I'm late. I gotta go now. I've

got directions to the sheriff's office. If there is anything new, I will call you."

Gabby looked up at Rafe. "I can't tell you what it means that you're here, Rafe. I know how busy you are." Gabby turned away from Rafe and walked over to the kitchen sink to wash her hands and throw away the paper towel.

"Of course I came. Iris is my niece. We're family, Gabby. I wouldn't be anywhere else. I need to leave now. I won't be long. I promise. Will you be okay while I'm gone?" He paused for a moment and brushed Gabby's hair back off her face.

Gabby looked up at her brother and wobbled a smile. "I'm gonna make cookies, right?"

Rafe kissed Gabby on the forehead. "That's my girl. I'll be back before you know it."

❧

No one looking at Oscar Stanley would guess at the depths of his depravity. His polished sophistication and dark, dangerous good looks fooled many to his true nature. He sat behind his desk. His gaze swept over the men in his office, who were part of his crew, with a look of disgust on his face.

"You left Louis alone with the merchandise? You know my brother can't be around little girls. If he damages the merchandise"—Oscar looked at Joey, his right-hand man, and drummed his fingers on the table—"I'll hold you responsible. Are we clear?"

Joey wiped his nose on the sleeve of his red flannel shirt. "Yeah, sure, boss."

"Good. Now, Mike, you make sure the transportation is set. You know what to do." Oscar jerked his head toward the door. "What are you waiting for?"

"Joey, you and Pete get your asses back to the cabin and make sure Louis doesn't do anything stupid. This is our most important mission, and I don't want any fuckups. Marco, you and I are going to make the ransom demand."

Oscar leaned back into his chair with a slight smile on his face. He'd show the big man. He was calling the shots now, and he hit Black Falls. It was a prime tourist trap, the perfect spot despite what the big man thought. *Yeah, I call the shots now.*

※

Iris scooted into the darkest corner of the cabin. If she were still enough, then maybe that dark-haired man with the mean brown eyes wouldn't find her. Dry blood crusted at her nose and soaked her torn shirt. Her exposed stomach showed bruised ribs. A faint imprint of a foot could be seen on her stomach. With head hid between her knees, Iris moaned. Tears drenched her face.

※

Rafe paced before the big bay window in the sheriff's office and ran a hand through his closely cropped hair. "Who is this woman, and what's taking her so long? I left my sister alone to meet this woman. Now where is she?"

Sheriff Jackson "Jack" Johnson was dressed in a casual

uniform of a blue button-down shirt, blue jeans, and cowboy boots. His badge was clipped over his left pocket. He wore a shoulder gun holster as he sat behind his desk with his hands behind his head. He took in Rafe Wolf's disheveled appearance and gave him a compassionate look from his sky-blue eyes. Before the sheriff could answer, a woman, diminutive in size, her curly black hair pulled back in a ponytail, holding what looked like a drawing pad, glanced at Rafe with a cool, assessing look from her sapphire-blue eyes.

"I'm nobody, Mr. Wolf," she said, holding his gaze. "Is everything set up for me, Jack?"

Her husky voice sent shivers down Rafe's spine, and his amber eyes glowed with a primal recognition as he returned her look.

Sheriff Johnson stood and gazed fondly at the woman. His gaze was warming. "Yes, everything is set up in the conference room for you."

The woman smiled at the sheriff and gave Rafe a lingering glance before she walked away.

Rafe rubbed the back of his neck and stood close to the desk. His jeans were suddenly a little too tight. *What the hell is wrong with me? My niece is missing. I don't have time for dreams remembered or evoked from just one look from this woman. God, I hope she's a woman.* She looked so tiny, swallowed up by the blue denim jacket she wore. Who knew how old she was.

Rafe turned to the sheriff and glared at him. His hands clenched into fists. "Are you kidding? You got me down here to meet some kid—a kid who can do what?" Rafe spit out.

"Don't let her size fool you. She's older than she looks, but more importantly, she finds people. We're going on ten hours here. Give her a chance," Jack said with a small smile.

Sally Ryan, a tall blonde in her late fifties who was the office manager and receptionist at the sheriff's office, knocked at the door and then walked into the office. "Jack, she's ready. She's asking for Randy to drive her. Do you want Joe and Denise to follow as backup?"

"Yeah, that sounds good. Joe is a great shot. Tell Randy and the others that it's a go. I want them in constant contact with me. Have them assess the situation and then call me," Jack said.

Sally smiled. "You got it, boss." She turned to leave.

"Sally, close the door, will you?" Jack asked.

"Sure thing, boss." Sally smiled as she closed the door behind her.

Rafe's eyes burned with anger. He lifted his fist, and through clenched teeth, he asked, "What the hell is going on here? What is a go? I want some answers."

Standing at six foot five, Sheriff Jack Johnson was an imposing figure. Silver was just beginning to show in his black hair. At age thirty-seven, he'd been in law enforcement for ten years and five years in the military before that. For seven of those ten years, he worked in a big city before he decided to come home. Working homicide in the city wore a man down.

Jack walked over to the coffee machine and poured himself a mug of coffee. "Coffee, Mr. Wolf?"

Rafe glared at Jack and slowly unclenched his fists. "Sure, I'll take some coffee." He realized that the sheriff would give him answers only once he got his anger under control. Rafe shook his head.

"How do you take your coffee?"

"Black is fine."

Jack sat down after handing Rafe his coffee. Rafe grimaced after taking a sip.

Jack smiled into his cup. "Not the best-tasting coffee, but it does the job. Look—I know this is a stressful situation, and I appreciate you agreeing to let me go outside of law enforcement to find your niece. Now, I can't tell you that I understand completely how Ms. Malone is able to find people like she does. She claims to be a finder, and if anyone can find your niece, it's her."

Rafe wearily sat down and slumped in the chair across from the sheriff. He hadn't slept since he left the city when his sister called to tell him his niece had been kidnapped. He was running out of patience.

"So you're not going to tell me anything." Rafe looked up from his mug. "Sheriff Johnson, my sister is devastated and stressed to the max. I should be with her. Instead I am here with you, and you're not telling me anything I didn't already know, except that you have some woman who claims to be a"—Rafe glared at the sheriff—"some kind of what? A finder and that she will find my niece."

Jack's phone rang, and he picked up on the second ring. "Johnson here. Yeah, Randy, what have you got? The Black Falls campground? Okay. Let me know what you find when you get there." Jack disconnected the call and looked over at Rafe. "My people believe that your niece may be at a cabin that has been closed for repairs at the local campground."

"Are you going to call the FBI and let them know about this abandoned cabin?" Rafe asked.

"Special Agent Steele was very much against us using Ms. Malone. I'll wait until we know how this lead pans out. I have good people working on this. As soon as I hear anything, I will let you know."

Rafe stood up and ran a hand over his face. "That's it! What is this woman doing that the FBI isn't?"

Jack sighed. "Look, Mr. Wolf ... Rafe ... just let us follow this lead, and I'll get back to you. Normally Ms. Malone never meets family members of a victim. I'm not really sure why she wanted to meet you. All I can tell you is that she's never been wrong." Jack took a sip of his coffee. "Let us follow this lead. Once my men have more information, I will call you. For now, go back to your sister's, and I'll contact you there."

Rafe clenched his hands into fists. "Fine. I don't know why I'm here. You could have told me all this over the phone, and I would not have left my sister all alone. She's baking cookies for Christ's sake. Now you tell me to go back to her house, and I know nothing new."

Jack stood up and rubbed the back of his neck. "Look. I know this is difficult. We are doing everything we can to find Iris, and Ms. Malone has just given us a new lead to follow. I don't understand why Ms. Malone needed to see you, but I do know that her methods work." Jack walked to the door. "Let us investigate this lead, and I will call you."

Rafe sighed. "Okay, I'll go to my sister's and wait to hear from you." He suddenly stopped and gripped the door. "This had better work, Johnson. I don't think my sister can take too much more. I don't want to get her hopes up only to crush them. So when you call, it had better be with real information and not some goose chase, where there is no new news or to say this Malone woman has failed to find Iris." Rafe stalked out of the door and slammed it behind him.

※

Jack walked back to his desk and sat back in his chair. He closed his eyes and wondered what the hell his cousin, Wynter Malone, was thinking, dragging in Rafe Wolf when she knew he had nothing new to tell him.

Jack grimaced. *God, I hope she has good news soon. Time is not on our side*, he thought with a sigh.

※

Wynter clutched Iris's teddy bear to her chest. Thank goodness Jack was able to get it from Gabby. She didn't always understand how her gift worked, but unless she had some connection to the person she was looking for or the individual she was helping, then she wouldn't be able to find the lost person or thing she was looking for. Finding things was easier as the person asking for the item to be found was usually the connection she needed. If the person didn't have a connection to the item lost, then it was difficult, if not impossible, to find the item he or she sought. She learned that the hard way.

Her stepfather had hated her gift, but that didn't mean he didn't use her gift to find things, like sunken treasure, for him. Finding people was harder. She had to find a way to connect with the lost person. Children were easier as they were more open and innocent. An item that the child was attached to usually gave her the connection she needed to find him or her. Her connection to Iris was telling her that she was hurt and in shock. She felt time was running out. Iris was in terrible physical danger, and the sooner she found her, the better.

Wynter looked at Deputy Randy Jeffers and gripped the teddy bear tighter. The deputy, an older man in his fifties, was in good physical shape. His military background stood him in good stead, as he was always calm in a crisis.

"Randy, please hurry. Something really bad will happen to Iris if we don't reach her soon."

Randy glanced at Wynter and nodded. "Don't worry, Wynter. We'll make it in time. Just hold on tight," he said as he stepped on the gas.

※

Rafe was looking out the window, and Gabby was wiping down the counter as they waited to hear from the sheriff. Brother and sister were similar in looks. Both had dark brown hair and amber-brown eyes. Their bronze skin reflected their Native American heritage. At six foot one, Rafe towered over his sister, who was slender and five foot seven.

Gabby came out from the kitchen. She walked over to Rafe and gripped his arm. "How much longer before we hear from the sheriff? John called and said he made the drop, but no one has shown up yet for the money. What's taking so long?"

Rafe put his arm around Gabby and hugged her. "These things take time. Why don't—"

Gabby pulled out of Rafe's arms and stalked back into the kitchen. "I'm not making any more cookies, Rafe. I just want my daughter back." Gabby put the teakettle on the stove and turned on the gas. "John is with the FBI at the drop site, and nothing is happening. We've done everything that the kidnappers wanted, and still nothing has happened." Gabby collapsed onto a stool at the kitchen counter and crossed her arms across her chest. "I just want my daughter back," she said brokenly.

Rafe sat next to Gabby and drew her against him. "I know, kiddo. I know."

Rafe's cell phone buzzed. He quickly pulled it out of his pocket and answered, "Wolf here." Rafe looked at Gabby. His face broke into a big grin. "Oh my God! I can't believe it! You found her. Mercy General. Yes, we'll be right there." He disconnected the call. "Gabby, they found Iris. That was Sheriff Johnson. They're taking her to Mercy General, and he wants us to meet them there. Call John. We need to go now."

Gabby burst into tears. "They found her. Oh my God! They found her."

※

Special Agent Derek Steele stormed into the waiting room of Mercy General and stood in front of Sheriff

Johnson, barely glancing at Rafe, who was seated next to the sheriff.

"What the hell's going on here, Johnson? You go Lone Ranger on my ass and don't keep me in the fucking loop. You could have done more harm than good."

Steele was impeccably dressed in a gray suit with a white shirt and blue-gray tie, which complemented his light gray eyes. Tall and lanky, what he lacked in bulk, he made up for with the force of his personality. He looked like he could have been an accountant rather than the hard-as-nails agent he was.

"You brought in some looney psychic. What the hell is wrong with you?"

Johnson stood up and put his hands into his pockets. "That so-called looney found Iris. She saved that little girl. I don't know what you're complaining about. The girl was found, and we have one of the kidnappers in custody."

"You don't know why I'm complaining?" Steele sputtered as he clenched his hands into fists. "This is my investigation. You have no idea what you have done. There was more to this case than just a kidnapped girl. You have ruined our chances of finding the head of this kidnapping ring with the stunt you've pulled."

Rafe stood up. "That little girl is my niece. You bet your ass she counts! What the hell are you talking about?"

Steele shook his head, took a deep breath, and looked at Rafe. "I apologize, Mr. Wolf. Of course your niece counts, and I'm glad we were able to find her and she's going to be okay. My unit and CARD is all about finding kidnapped children and bringing them home safely. Unfortunately there was another aspect to this case." Steele glared at

Johnson. "One hour, Johnson. Your office," Steele said as he turned and walked away.

Jack looked at Rafe and shrugged his shoulders. "I better go and straighten things out with Special Agent Steele. I'm glad your niece was found. I'll stop by later and see if Iris has remembered anything more about the men who took her. If you need anything, just call me." Jack picked up his hat and walked out.

***

Jack sat behind his dark mahogany desk. A frown marred his brow. "You called this meeting, Steele."

Steele glared at Jack. He turned his back on him and walked over to the bay window. His teeth clenched. "We included you in this case because the kidnapping happened in your town. We gave you every courtesy, yet when you got information, you deliberately left me out of the loop. We're trying to break a kidnapping ring here. It wasn't just about finding the Richardses' kid. We're trying to find the mastermind behind all these kidnappings. This is more than kidnapping."

Steele sighed and turned to look at Jack. "These kidnappers sell these kids to the highest bidders. We identified the one kidnapper we arrested. A few months ago, we caught a break in another kidnapping case, and we learned one man is controlling small crews of three to five men. These crews operate all over the country, kidnapping children and then selling them as sex slaves. Before we could find out more about the man at the top, our informant was killed. No ransom has ever been demanded before. Dammit, these parents and the uncle scrambled to get the money together. Then nothing, a no-show at the pickup site. I thought this break in MO would be the break we needed to catch the sick bastard who is masterminding these abductions."

Jack leaned forward. "Look, you say you gave me every courtesy, but you didn't tell me about a kidnapping or child trafficking ring. Even so, I don't see how rescuing Iris Richards could have hindered your case. We have one of the kidnappers in custody. You can still get information from him."

Steele walked over and stood in front of Jack's desk, looking down at him. "You're right. We have one of the kidnappers, but he's lawyered up. He's a dead end for now." Steele's cell phone buzzed. He looked at the number and sighed. "I need to take this," Steele said as he turned away from Jack. "Steele here." He frowned, swore, and then disconnected the call.

Steele turned back to Jack. "That was one of my people. It seems that our kidnapper was shanked in jail. Our best lead is dead, just like last time." He sat down and placed his forearms on his knees with his head down as he softly cursed. "Just plain bad luck. That's all we've had. We think we are finally getting somewhere. Then bam! Our best lead gets himself killed."

Jack sat back and rubbed his forehead. "I don't know what to say. My focus was on finding the kidnapper and returning Iris Richards to her parents, which I did. I'm sorry if you feel like I've stepped on your toes. I'm sorry we couldn't get any information from that scumbag before he was killed. I'm not going to apologize for finding

Iris. I really don't see how finding Iris impeded your investigation."

Steele glanced at Jack. "Look, you made the right call. Finding the kid, well, that is everything. We were hoping the kidnappers would pick up the money so we could trace it. These bastards are smart. The ransom money was a new development. I don't know what it was. It could have been a diversion, or something else happened, and the kidnappers weren't able to collect the ransom."

Steele shook his head. "There's a pattern here, but we just haven't figured it out. These guys have run my team ragged. It took us a while to see a connection to these kidnappings. Leaving a ransom was new, and we thought we might finally get a break in the case. Must be one hell of a psychic you got there. Lucky for Iris that you found her. Otherwise she would just be gone, vanished without a trace, just like all the others. Maybe your psychic can tell us where this gang is hiding out?" Steele said with a tired smile.

"You said they didn't pick up the money. Maybe they knew you were on to them and that is why they didn't pick up the money," Jack said.

Steele slammed his fist on Jack's desk. "Fuck, just when we thought we'd gotten a break in the case, this guy gets himself killed." Steele slumped back into his chair and sighed. "Well, maybe next time we'll get that break."

"Next time?" Jack asked.

"With this gang, there seems to always be a next time," Steele said. "Maybe you were right. Maybe they knew we had trackers on the money. I ... well ... I guess we can call this a win. Just wish we'd gotten more information regarding the ringleader."

Jack gave Steele a weary smile "Sometimes we barely make a dent. Take what you can get. We saved the kid."

"I hate that we have to wait for another kidnapping to happen so we can get new evidence, hoping that this crew will fuck it up somehow." Steele turned and put his hands in his pockets. "How many kids ... well, I just ... well, I know you're right. Iris Richards is home. I hate knowing there will be another kidnapping and I can't do anything to stop it. These guys, whoever they are, are good."

Quietly Steele left Jack's office.

※

Rafe sat alone in the waiting room at Mercy General with his long legs stretched out before him as he stared at the ceiling. John Richards, a good-looking man with light blond hair and green eyes, came out of Iris's room and walked toward his brother-in-law.

"Hey, Rafe," John said. He looked down at his shoes with his face grim and his hands jammed into his pants pockets. "Christ, those bastards drugged and beat my little girl. The doctors said she wasn't raped, but she's hurt and confused. She doesn't remember anything."

John ran his hand through his hair. "The doctors say she could regain her memory, but God, I hope she doesn't. She's six, man. I mean, what kind of monster kidnaps and beats a little girl?" John sat down next to Rafe. "I don't know what to say. I was against using the psychic, but if it weren't for her ..."

Rafe shrugged. "I'm just glad Iris was found before anything else happened to her. She's safe now, and that is all that matters. When can you take her home?"

John smiled tiredly. "Today. We're just waiting on the discharge papers."

※

Oscar stood by the window in his richly decorated office. His face was beaded with sweat and red. "What the fuck happened? My brother Louis is dead, and the girl was rescued. Mike, what the hell happened to our transportation? In and out, that's how we run a job. We leave no prints, nothing. Louis is dead, and his DNA is all over the place. This was our biggest job."

He slammed his fist against the wall and winced. "Fuck, now we had to leave the ransom. Joey, shut everything down now. We need to get outta here fast and hope the big boss doesn't learn of this fuckup." Oscar wiped the sweat off his face. "Christ, what the fuck happened? Joey, you find out what the fuck went wrong."

2

Six Months Later

RAFE FINALLY REACHED HIS sister's house in Black Falls after a two-hour drive. It was a small, sleepy coastal town on the East Coast. He couldn't believe that he was actually moving here. Small-town life would be a big change from living in New York City. He'd had enough of it, and he was looking to simplify his life. Finally that nightmare was done. He still couldn't believe that his partner was skimming money from their firm. Black Falls was just what he needed. He'd be closer to his family and could start over, running his own practice. Thankfully he could stay with his sister until he could find a place of his own.

Rafe pulled into the driveway and looked at his sister's two-story, white colonial with its black shutters. The leaves were vibrant with color. Autumn was his favorite season with its colorful bounty and cooler weather. Rafe got out of his hunter green Jeep Cherokee and took a deep breath. He straightened his jeans and pushed up the sleeves of his brown cable-knit sweater. The crisp air was refreshing. As he walked toward the house, the front door was thrown open, and a little whirlwind, dressed in jeans and a pink sweatshirt with a unicorn on it, ran out of the house.

"Uncle Rafe! Uncle Rafe, you're here!" Iris said as she threw herself into Rafe's waiting arms.

Rafe caught her in his arms and smiled at her, giving her a hug. Iris took after his side of the family with her dark brown hair and bronze complexion. Her green eyes were the only feature she got from her father, John. "Hey, squirt, how's my favorite niece?"

Iris giggled and hugged Rafe. "I gotta A on my drawing. You wanna see?" Before he could answer, the seven-year-old had squirmed out of his arms and ran into the house.

"Sure, princess," Rafe murmured as he followed Iris into the house.

"No running in the house, sunshine," John said to his daughter as she ran by him.

Rafe grinned at John. "Hey, I really appreciate you letting me stay with you until I can get a place of my own. The bulk of my stuff is in storage, but I brought some things with me. I hope you don't mind."

John ran a hand through his hair, making it stand up on end. "No problem, man. I'm hoping your presence will help your sister. Ever since, well, you know, it's like she's become a different person. All she does is obsess about Iris and her safety." John shook his head. "The extra money will come in handy as well. I'm not saying business is bad, but with all these therapy and counseling fees piling up on top of each other, it will be nice to get a little breathing room. Come on in. You're just in time for dinner," John said as he made his way into the house.

"How's Iris doing? Is she still having nightmares? Has she remembered anything from that day?" Rafe asked as he followed John into the house.

"Iris is doing better, but yeah, she still has nightmares. And no, she still hasn't remembered anything yet. This new psychologist she's been seeing believes that part of the reason Iris is still having such intense nightmares is because her memories are trying to break free. Right now, it's Gabby who worries me the most. I'm … I think …"

John shrugged his shoulders. "Gabby monitors Iris's every move. She makes Iris wear a tracking device when she leaves the house. She feels guilty that Iris was taken, even though it wasn't her fault. So now she watches Iris's every move. She won't let her go over to other kids' houses, even wearing the tracking device. It's only been recently that she let Iris go back to school. She has baby monitors all over the house. She barely trusts her with me. It's starting to affect Iris. She's acting out at school, but well, I guess it's natural for everything that she's been through, what we've all been through. I love your sister, but things have been tense. Hopefully this new therapist will help."

Rafe took a good look at his brother-in-law. John was dressed casually in jean shorts, a dark green sweatshirt that complemented his green eyes, and sneakers. Looking at him now, it would be difficult to tell he was a successful chef and businessman, running his own restaurant. He looked like a surfer dude with his tan and light blond hair. John had aged in the past year. The lines in his face were a little deeper.

"I hope it helps as well. Now that I'm here, maybe the two of you can get away for a while and reconnect."

John sighed. "Don't count on it. Gabby won't even go to the grocery store unless Iris is with her. But enough about that. Gabby's in the kitchen, so why don't you go say hello, and I'll get us some drinks." John walked to the back porch, where an outside refrigerator held soda and beer.

Rafe walked into the kitchen. Gabby was pulling out a piping-hot pan of baked ziti, which she set on the counter next to some garlic bread. As Rafe's gaze raked over her, he noted that she had lost weight. Her jeans and blue V-neck sweater hung loosely off her body, emphasizing her newfound thinness.

"Hey, Gabby."

Gabby took off her oven mitts and rushed to hug her brother. "Rafe! I'm so happy you're here. Did you see Iris? Doesn't she look wonderful?"

"Slow down, Gabby," Rafe said with a smile, enveloping her within his warm hug. "Yes, I have seen Iris, and yes, she looks wonderful. How are you, kiddo?"

"Good, good," Gabby said as she looked up at Rafe and smiled.

Iris ran into the kitchen, holding a drawing in her hand. "Uncle Rafe, look. Here's my drawing."

Rafe took the drawing from Iris, surprised by the

detail and quality of the picture. "It's beautiful, princess. Just beautiful."

"Enough, you two. Iris, go put your drawing away. I'm about to put dinner on the table. And don't forget to wash your hands. Go on," Gabby said. "Rafe, please put the baked ziti on the table. I'll be right out with the salad and bread."

※

"Iris is all tucked in for the night." Gabby sat down at the dining room table. She reached over, checked the monitor, and then set it next to her.

John looked over at Rafe, nodding toward the baby monitor.

"So I have circled some houses that are for sale for you to look at," Gabby said as she handed Rafe the real estate section of the newspaper.

Rafe laughed. "In a hurry to get rid of me, sis?"

Gabby blushed. "No, I just thought—"

"I'm teasing you, Gabby. You need to lighten up a little bit." Rafe reached over and tweaked Gabby's nose.

Gabby pushed away her brother's hand, dropped her gaze to stare into her wineglass, and swirled the liquid around. "It's so good to have you here, Rafe." Gabby's eyes gleamed with unshed tears.

Rafe smiled at his sister. "I'm happy to be here, kiddo. A fresh start is just what I need."

"What a shock! What was George thinking? He must have known he would get caught stealing from the firm," John said as he reached for his beer and took a sip.

"Shock doesn't even begin to describe it. I knew he liked to gamble, but—" Rafe shrugged.

"Now he's in prison. I thought he was such a nice man," Gabby said.

"After ten years, you would think I would have known how serious his gambling problem was. If only he would have come to me, I would have gladly helped him out," Rafe said.

"He probably felt ashamed," John said.

Gabby looked at her brother with a mischievous gleam in her eye. "Not to change the subject, but you know, Rafe, I think I have found the perfect girl for you."

"What! Now wait a minute. I'm just getting over what happened with George. I'm buying into a new law practice. The last thing I need right now is a new woman in my life," Rafe said with a laugh, holding up his hands in mock surrender.

Gabby turned to John and winked at him. "Don't you think Wynter is just perfect for Rafe?"

John laughed. "Now that would be a match."

Rafe scowled at his sister. "I can find my own woman. Thank you very much."

Gabby smirked at Rafe. "We'll see, big brother. We'll see."

※

Rafe plopped back onto his bed. *God, I am exhausted from the emotional wringer I've been put through for the past year. First it was the kidnapping. Then it was George stealing from the firm to pay his gambling debts, and now this move to Black*

Falls. He sighed as he rubbed his eyes. *Yes, a new start,* he thought with a yawn.

He turned off the light and settled into bed. Rafe fell into a deep sleep and eagerly entered into the dream world where she awaited him. He felt exquisite pleasure as she ran her fingers down his chest, sliding over his thigh to his throbbing shaft. He stared into the most beautiful blues eyes he'd ever seen. Though he dreamed of her many times, he still did not know her name, but he knew he knew her. She lowered her head and gently caressed his lips with hers. He lifted his hands and tangled them in her hair as he deepened the kiss. Her fingers grasped him, enflaming his desire.

"Angel, if you keep that up, it will be over before we've had a chance to begin."

She looked up at him and smiled. "This is my time, lover, and I love making you lose control." She ran her tongue down his throat to his chest and swirled it around his nipple, making it pebble.

Rafe groaned. Rafe cupped her breast and lightly pinched her nipple. Lowering his head, he took her nipple into his mouth and gently suckled it, loving the sweet sounds that his lover made. "God, I love your sweet taste."

Her midnight curls teased his chest as she moved lower, kissing her way down his body. She dragged her tongue across the tip of his penis.

Rafe arched into her sweet kiss and moaned. "Babe, if you continue on this way, it will be over too soon."

Rafe pulled her up and took her mouth in a scorching kiss. He ran his hand down her body and stroked her wet heat. She was so ready for him. He rolled her beneath him and—

A scream pierced through the haze of pleasure. Rafe jolted upright on the bed and looked around wildly. *What the fuck*, he thought. *Damn, I'm hard as a rock and drenched in sweat.*

Rafe jumped out of bed as he heard a commotion outside his bedroom door. He pulled on his sweatpants and opened the bedroom door. He saw John trailing behind Gabby, who rushed into Iris's room.

"What's happened?" Rafe scratched his chest and yawned.

John rubbed his face. "Iris had another nightmare. Damn, it's been a few days and … well, I was hopeful that the damn things were gone. Gabby will calm her down, but Iris does better when we both are there after one of her nightmares. It will take a while for her to calm down and go back to sleep."

Rafe yawned again. "Is there anything I can do?"

"Nah, Iris will soon go back to sleep. I just wish … look, man, I'm sorry she woke you up. There really isn't much we can do. The doctor says all we can do is be there for her and the dreams should start to lessen in intensity and frequency in time." John sighed and shook his head. "I just feel so damn helpless. My baby is hurting, and I can't do anything to make it better for her."

Rafe looked at John's tired face and sighed. "I'm gonna make some hot chocolate for Gabby and pour us a couple of brandies. I'll meet you both in the kitchen."

"Thanks, Rafe. A brandy would be nice, and I'm sure Gabby would love a hot chocolate. We should be down in a few." John forced a smile on his face as he walked into his daughter's room.

※

Across town, Wynter sat up in bed and frowned. Something was wrong. Her dream lover left their dream abruptly. That never happened before. Knowing sleep would be elusive, Wynter got up and padded downstairs into the kitchen. A cup of chamomile was just what she needed. Rufus, a fawn-colored mastiff, had followed her downstairs.

"You want to go out, boy? It's a beautiful night."

Sitting on the porch swing, wrapped in a quilt, Wynter wondered when she and her dream lover would connect again. Though she loved their dreaming, she needed more. She sighed as she stared at the stars above.

3

Jack sat in a booth in the back of the Blue Diner waiting for his cousin. The diner in the center of town was a good place to pick up local gossip. A slender waitress in her early forties with dyed blonde hair was dressed in a blue T-shirt with the name of the diner done in white lettering. She wore blue jeans and had a half-white apron tied around her waist.

She approached Jack. "Good morning, sweetie. Do you want your usual?"

Jack smiled and winked. "You know it, Daisy. Also, can you bring a cup of Earl Grey with honey?"

Daisy and her husband, Hank, a big bear of a man, who was usually found in the kitchen, owned the Blue Diner. Jack and Hank grew up together, and when Hank had the chance to buy the diner, Jack put up some of the money and became a silent partner.

"You got it, darling," Daisy said as she turned to place the order.

The bell rang above the door as it opened, and his cousin, Wynter Malone, walked in. Her curly black hair was piled on top of her head with a few wisps framing her delicate heart-shaped face. Beautiful sapphire-blue eyes gazed at him as she sat down across from him. She was dressed casually in a white T-shirt with a blue flannel shirt over it, worn blue jeans, and scruffy brown hiking boots. She was beautiful, if one could overlook the thin, white scar that ran down the length of the left side of her face, starting from the corner of her eye and running down to her chin.

His heart always broke a little when he saw her. She always seemed so alone. Like all the women of his family, Wynter was psychic, and her gift often made it difficult for her to let people in. Every woman in his family had dreams of her one true love. He'd known that Wynter dreamed of Rafe Wolf. He just hoped this Wolf guy realized his good fortune. Wynter deserved some happiness in her life. He hoped Wynter would finally let someone in and accept love.

"I ordered you an Earl Grey with honey," Jack said.

"Thanks, Jack. So what's this about?" Wynter asked as she sat across from Jack.

"I hear Rafe Wolf is back in town, that he's looking to buy a house and settle here. Rumor has it that he bought into old man Jeffrey's practice," Jack said.

Wynter pulled the sleeves of her shirt over her hands. "Yeah, I heard. I know Mr. Jeffrey wants to retire in a couple of years to be closer to his wife's family in Florida." She gazed at her cousin. "We knew he would be back."

"Hey, Wynter," Daisy interrupted. "Here's your Earl

Grey and the breakfast special for you, Jack. Do y'all need anything else?"

"Naw, we're good for now, Daisy." Jack looked over his plate and licked his lips.

Wynter looked at Jake's plate of eggs over easy, bacon, hash browns, and pancakes and grimaced. "How you can eat all that is beyond me. How do you stay so fit?"

"It's all in the genes, cuz. You should know," Jack said and smiled.

Wynter shuddered. "Whatever, dude."

Jack frowned down at his food. "So you're okay with this Rafe character moving here?"

Wynter took a sip of her tea. "You know I dream, Jack."

"Yeah, yeah, so you dream. How do you feel about it? You can't let a dream dictate your life. I don't care what my mom says," Jack said.

Wynter sighed. "I don't know, Jack. I guess we'll just have to wait and see what happens."

4

Oscar stood at the window in his office, sipping a whisky neat. "What have you found out, Joey?"

Joey wiped the sweat from his forehead. "Nuttin new, boss. Nobody knows nuttin about that Black Falls job. What's the big deal anyways? It happened over six months ago."

Oscar clenched his jaw and slammed his fist on his desk. "Why is this important? How about we might have a rat among us? How about my brother was killed because of this? I want to know what went wrong. I want to know how that sheriff knew where that kid was, and I want to know now. You talk to that local guy who helped us. Do you understand me, Joey?"

"Yeah, boss. I understand," Joey said, swallowing hard.

"What the hell are you doing standing around here? Get outta here, you idiot," Oscar said, shaking his head.

The boss had them running ragged ever since the Black Falls job. He needed to know what went wrong with that job. He needed to know who was responsible for his brother's death.

5

Wynter parked her black VW convertible bug in front of Rosie's Good Reads and Café. Rosie had called to let her know that the new Kevin Hearne book was out. Wynter breathed deeply and enjoyed the feel of the sun on her face. It was a beautiful crisp day, a perfect time to curl up in her favorite chair with a cup of hot cocoa and read a good book. Wynter turned to open the door and bumped into what felt like a brick wall.

"Umph! What the—" Wynter gasped. She craned her neck and met the amused gaze of Rafe Wolf.

"Hello. It's Ms. Malone, right?" Rafe asked as he felt like a brick just hit him in the head.

Shit, she is my dream girl. I'd know those blue eyes anywhere, he thought.

Wynter bit her lower lip as she felt a familiar stirring of her senses. *God, he looks so much better in person than he does in my dreams. He takes my breath away*, Wynter thought.

"Ummm, Wynter. My name is Wynter," she said with her eyes glued to his face. She touched her lips, remembering the passionate kisses they shared in her dreams.

Rafe couldn't look away from her mouth. *God, the things that mouth …*

Rafe shook his head, trying to clear his thoughts. "It's my pleasure." He inhaled, breathing in her scent. His eyes were hot with desire.

Wynter was mesmerized and felt herself falling into his gaze. She reached up to meet his lips in a kiss. She couldn't believe how turned on she was. Just the thought of kissing him had her panties damp.

"Excuse me," a teenage girl said as she moved around them to go into the bookstore.

They broke apart. A red flush enflamed Wynter's cheeks. "Are you going into the bookstore?" Wynter stammered.

"Bookstore?" Rafe asked, dazed.

Wynter nodded her head toward the door. "Yes, the bookstore. A new book came out from one of my favorite authors." She took a deep breath and looked down at her beat-up old boots.

"Ahh, yeah, the bookstore. I'm here to pick up a book for my niece," Rafe said.

With her breathing evening out, Wynter looked up at Rafe. "How's Iris doing?"

"Good, good," Rafe said as he opened the door to the bookstore for Wynter. "I never did get the chance to thank you."

Wynter bit her lip. "There's no need to thank me. I'm

just glad that we found Iris and that everything turned out okay." Wynter looked up at Rafe as they walked into the bookstore. "I'd really appreciate it if you didn't say anything about my involvement in finding Iris." Wynter pulled at the neck of her blue sweater.

Rafe frowned. "Sure, no problem. Umm …"

Wynter looked up at him quizzically.

"Hey, you want to go out for dinner tomorrow night?" Rafe silently sighed.

Real smooth, Wolf. Real smooth, he thought.

"Oh! Ookay!" Wynter stammered, caught off guard by the question. She pushed her hair off her face.

"How about I pick you up at six?" Rafe said, smiling at Wynter's reaction.

"Six, great. I'll see you then," Wynter said as she grabbed her book and headed for the cash register. "Gabby knows where I live. Ask her for directions," she said over her shoulder.

Rafe watched Wynter leave, feeling shocked.

God, I found my dream woman, he thought.

※

"So what do you know about Wynter Malone?" Rafe asked his sister. They were at John and Gabby's house, sitting at the dining room table drinking Irish coffees.

Gabby leaned back in her chair and glanced at the baby monitor. "You know Wynter Malone?" Gabby's eyebrows shot up.

"Yeah, I ran into her today at the bookstore," Rafe said

and smiled at Gabby. His cheeks reddened as his thoughts raced to his dreams.

Oh yeah, I know Wynter, he thought.

"I asked her out to dinner for tomorrow night."

"Oh, Rafe, that is wonderful news. Wynter seems like such a wonderful girl. She's great with Iris. I just knew you would like her," Gabby gushed, smirking at her husband. "See, I told you that Rafe would like Wynter."

John laughed. "Okay, you win. He likes Wynter."

"How do you know Wynter?" Rafe asked.

"Well, Wynter is giving Iris art lessons. She really helped Iris, not only with her drawing, but well, since Iris has been taking lessons from Wynter, she seems to be more like herself, if you know what I mean?" Gabby said. "She laughs when she is with Wynter."

"Wynter's an art teacher?" Rafe asked.

"No. Wynter is an artist, but she agreed to give Iris lessons. She isn't a teacher or anything like that." Gabby took a sip of her irish coffee. "So where are you going to take her tomorrow?"

Rafe looked at his brother-in-law, and he gave him a blank stare. "I … I guess …"

John smiled at the look of panic on Rafe's face. "Why don't you take her to the restaurant?" John took a sip of his drink. "This could be good. I hired a new chef, and you can tell me how you like the food."

"The restaurant. Yes, that would be perfect. Thanks, John. You're a real lifesaver." Rafe sighed, smiled at John, and relaxed back into his chair. "Perfect."

Rafe fisted his hands in the sheets of his bed.

"Dad, what are you doing?" Rafe watched helplessly as his father drew a gun from the back of his pants. "Dad, what the fuck?"

Slowly his father lifted the gun and put the muzzle of the gun into his mouth. He looked directly at Rafe and pulled the trigger.

Rafe woke with a start, choking back the scream that clogged his throat. *God, how I hate this nightmare*, he thought. Maybe Iris's nightmare triggered his. It had been a while since he dreamed that particular dream. *Will I ever stop dreaming of my father's death?* he wondered.

Hatred for his old man bubbled within him, leaving a sour taste in his mouth. Rafe wiped the sweat from his brow and reached for the bottle of water on the nightstand next to his bed. He guzzled the water, grimaced, and wiped his mouth with the back of his hand. He couldn't understand how his mother had put up with his father's drunken ways. *If only I hadn't walked my father's dream.* He and his sister wouldn't have been forced to live with his grandfather on the reservation. The only good aspect of his gift was the dreams he shared with his lover. And he prayed nothing bad would come from them.

He turned to his pillow and punched it a couple of times. With his arm under his head, he leaned back against his pillow. *Just what I need, another sleepless night*, he thought.

6

Wynter sat at the dining room table at her aunt and uncle's house. Her aunt Helen always reminded her of those hippies who believed in flower power. Her curly black hair, streaked with gray, was loose around her shoulders. She wore a red muumuu dress with white jasmine flowers on it, as well as big leaf earrings and red beads.

She looked around, enjoying the plants that littered the room. Helen had an affinity with plants. Everything grew when she was around. She was an herbalist who knew the healing properties of plants and made natural remedies for those in need, along with natural skin care products.

Her uncle Stuart, a tall man with gray hair, had a bit of a paunch. He looked comfortable in his khaki pants, green shirt, and sweater vest. In his sixties, he was still actively working at his nursery every day. His deep green eyes were sharp and missed little.

Her aunt and uncle had taken her in when it was discovered that her stepfather was abusing her. Their home reflected warmth and love. Knickknacks were on the mantle, and books were stuffed into bookcases. Plants and family photos were on every available surface. It was a safe haven for a young girl of eleven whose world changed dramatically when her mother died, leaving her with a stepfather who thought she was a freak and did his best to beat the devil out of her.

"Aunt Helen, the lasagna was wonderful," Wynter said as she pushed away her plate.

Helen smiled, and her eyes gleamed with humor. "Thank you, honey. I know it's your favorite." Helen gave Wynter a long look. "I hear you bumped into that good-looking brother of Gabby Richards."

Wynter blushed. "Yes," she said as she folded her napkin. "We're, ummm, going out tomorrow for dinner."

"Good for you, honey. It's about time," Stuart said as he looked at Wynter over the top of his glasses.

"Are you dreaming?" Helen picked up her wineglass and swirled the wine around.

Wynter shrugged. "You know I am."

"And is he the man you are dreaming about?"

Wynter sniffed. "You know he is."

"Aw, honey, you know the women of this family always have dreams of their one true love. I just want you to be happy, honey. You deserve it." Helen put down her glass and reached over to squeeze Wynter's hand.

Wynter frowned. "What if?" Wynter looked at her aunt. A frown marred her brow. "What if he can't accept my gift?" she whispered.

Helen shared a nervous glance with Stuart. "He's your dream man, honey. I'm sure he'll be able to accept your gift," Helen said and squeezed Wynter's hand again.

She always worried about Wynter. She was often too quiet, holding things in, keeping herself separate, always afraid of being rejected. She cursed Wynter's stepfather, Neil, who made her life a living hell.

When did anyone besides my aunt's family ever accept my gift and me? Wynter thought. Though her aunt and cousin Sara thought their psychic abilities were gifts, Wynter didn't see it that way. *People think I'm a freak, and they're right*, she thought as she rubbed her scar.

※

Helen was curled up on the living room couch, sipping raspberry tea with honey. She didn't know what to make of the call she got from her sister Marguerite.

Stuart came into the living room and sat next to his wife. "What's wrong, hon?"

"I got a strange call from Marguerite."

"What she have to say?"

Helen took a sip of her tea and then put her cup down on the coffee table. She turned to her husband and grasped his hand in her own. "You know Marguerite. It's vague, but from what I gather, Wynter may be in some kind of danger, and her father may be involved."

Stuart squeezed his wife's hand. "That no-good bastard. When did he get back in town? And why hasn't Charles called? Whenever his big wheeling-dealing cousin is back in town, he always crows about it, kowtowing to him as if he were royalty or something. You'd think he'd have figured out by now what scum his cousin really is. What kind of awful scheme could he be involved in that would put Wynter in danger?"

Helen rubbed her thumb across her husband's hand and sighed. "I don't know, dear, but my guess is it's something really bad. Marguerite believes he's a danger to Wynter and that something bad is going to happen real soon." Helen shuddered and burrowed into Stuart's embrace. "Do you think it's time to tell Wynter about her father? I know we promised Brenna we wouldn't tell Wynter about her father, but—"

Stuart squeezed his wife into a tighter hug. "Let's wait and see what happens. If there is any possible way to keep that bastard away from Wynter, the better off she'll be. Brenna had good reasons for not wanting Wynter to know about her father."

Helen sighed. "You're right. He's dangerous and unpredictable. No one had worst taste in men than my baby sister Brenna. Let's wait and see what happens."

※

Wynter was sitting at the kitchen table at her childhood home. He pointed to the map before her. "Tell me. Tell me where the treasure is, you demon from hell."

He pulled her head back by her hair and forced her to look at him. Blood dripped down her cheek. "Your mother isn't here to protect you now, bitch. I'll scar more than your face. Now tell me where the treasure is. This is the original map. I know you can find it."

Suddenly someone started pounding on the door. "Neil, open this door. I know you are in there, and I know you are hurting Wynter. Open this door now!" Stuart Johnson shouted.

Neil Malone slammed Wynter's head on the table. "This isn't over, bitch. You will tell me where that treasure is."

"Neil, I have Sheriff Richards with me. Open this door, or we will break the door in," Stuart yelled.

Neil drew back his hand and fisted it. Wynter screamed. The kitchen door crashed open as Stuart and the sheriff burst into the room.

Wynter woke up drenched in sweat to her own screams. She pushed her damp hair off her face and grabbed the bottle of water on her nightstand, gulping it as she tried to shake off her nightmare.

It's only a dream. He can't hurt me any longer, she thought. Her stepfather was dead, and he couldn't hurt her anymore.

Rufus settled in next to her. She put her arms around him in a tight hug.

"Don't worry, boy. I'll be okay. It's just a bad dream. Only a dream," she murmured against him as she tried to decide who she was trying to convince, her or her dog. Wynter shivered and buried her face against Rufus's neck.

※

John and Rafe sat on the back porch. The crickets were singing, and both were enjoying a whiskey.

John looked over at Rafe and frowned. "I know Gabby

is thrilled that you are going out with Wynter, and I'm not saying that Wynter isn't a good person, but I grew up here. Her family has always been different. I mean, people flock to that aunt of hers for remedies, thinking she can cure their ailments. I even heard they go to her for love potions or some such nonsense. Not that I have ever heard anything about Wynter, but they say magic runs through the female line of the family."

Rafe shivered, and his eye twitched as he took a sip of his drink. "What are you saying? That these people are con artists?"

John shook his head. "No, that's not what I'm saying. All I'm saying is that they are a little bit different. I mean, the sheriff is a good man and does his job well. And I always respected Stuart Johnson, his dad, but there have been some wild stories about the women of that family. Just be careful. That's all."

Rafe's brow went up. "What does the sheriff have to do with Wynter and her family?"

John gave him a strange look. "Jack Johnson is Wynter's cousin. His family took her in when she was a kid. After her mother died, it was discovered that her stepfather was abusing her. He claimed he was trying to save her, trying to beat the devil out of her. That's how she got that scar on her face."

"What about her father? Where was he when all of this was going on?" Rafe scowled down at his drink, not liking where this conversation was going.

"Don't know," John said and frowned. "Come to think of it, I don't think anyone knows who her father is. There has been speculation, but that's a secret her mother took to the grave. Look, all I'm saying is to be careful." John then sighed.

Rafe nodded and shuddered as dark memories from his past surfaced. He didn't really need complications in his life right now.

※

Rafe leaned backed against the headboard of his bed. He turned to fluff his pillows, trying to get comfortable. He sighed and picked up the book he had been trying to read. He sighed again and put the book down again. He wasn't ready to face his dreams. Yes, he loved the dreams he shared with Wynter. A shiver of pleasure ran down his spine, and his body hardened as he remembered the eroticism of those dreams. *What that woman does to my body.*

He never felt such intense emotions as those that Wynter stirred within him. He frowned, wondering if his dreams with Wynter were as harmful as his dream walking. *My gift? No, my curse.*

Rafe rubbed his eyes. No, he was not going to go down that road. He found out the hard way that dream walking was dangerous. He shook his head. What he shared with Wynter was different. No, those dreams weren't dangerous. Rafe looked at his book, uttered a curse, and threw it on the nightstand. Sighing, he turned off the light and gave himself over to his dreams.

7

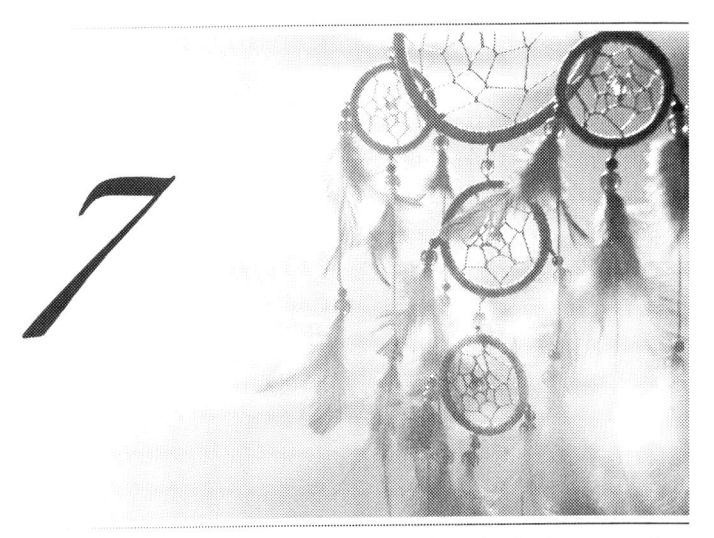

Wynter shivered as she thrashed about in her bed. The monster was back, and it wanted another child. Wynter moaned as she tried to protect the boy.

"Nooo, you can't have him!" Wynter woke up screaming.

God, not again, she thought, *not another dream about kidnappings.*

Wynter struggled to untangle herself from the sweat-ridden sheets entwined around her body. *What the hell?* She never dreamed of someone being kidnapped. Something was lost. She could find it. Someone went missing. She could probably find him or her. She didn't dream about the person becoming lost.

And what good was this dream anyway, some vague images and a horrible feeling of dread? Deep breaths. In and out. Just breathe, she thought. *Am I losing my mind? Too much stress?*

Slowly Wynter sat up and leaned back against her

pillow. Her T-shirt clung to her damp body. The dream did have a familiar feel to it. *Could it be the same kidnappers who took Iris?* she thought. Pushing her wet curls from her face, she reached for the phone.

❀

Jack poured himself a cup of coffee and handed Wynter a cup of Earl Grey tea with honey as they sat at the kitchen table.

"No details of when this kidnapping will happen or who the kidnappers are?" Jack asked.

Wynter gripped her cup of tea in both hands. "No. Just that another kidnapping will happen," she said as she shivered. "God, Jack, am I losing my mind? I've never dreamed like this before. Sure, I've dreamed of my dream man, but this … I hate this dream. It's the second time I've had it. I only get vague images and a feeling of dread. I know someone is going to be kidnapped, but who? And I have a feeling it will be the same kidnappers who were involved in Iris's kidnapping, whoever they are."

Jack rubbed the back of his neck. "Tell me again what you saw."

Wynter ran a hand through her unruly curls. "Jack, we've been over it a hundred times. There is nothing else I can tell you. The monster …" Wynter shivered. "Well, he's in the shadows, but I can feel his glee. He loves terrorizing children. It was so cold and so dark in the dream. I couldn't see anything. I just …"

Wynter took a sip of her tea. "I just couldn't see anything. I only felt his hate and the pleasure he took in terrorizing the child. The rest were just impressions. You know how dreams can go. I only caught glimpses of things."

Jack frowned. A faraway look was in his eyes. "Did you get an idea of what this man looked like? Did you see any distinguishing features?"

"No, I just got the impression that he was big, but in a dream, that doesn't necessarily mean he is literally big."

"How big are we talking? I mean Rufus towers over you when he stands on his hind legs," Jack joked, trying to wipe the sad and scared look from his cousin's face.

"Rufus is a freaking mastiff, Jack. Of course he towers over me. I know you think I am short, but five foot two is not all that short," Wynter huffed as she rubbed Rufus behind his ear. "Is it, boy?"

Jack laughed. "Okay, shorty, settle down." The smile left his face. "I guess we'll just have to wait and see what happens. Maybe you'll have another dream. Do you want me to stay with you tonight?"

Wynter got up, put her empty cup in the sink, and nodded her head. "Yeah, if it's not too much of a bother? I would really love for you to stay." Wynter shivered. "Don't worry. I cleaned the guest room the other day." Wynter shook her head. Her eyes darted around the room. "I got that date tomorrow night. What if … what if he can't handle my gift? I mean, look at me. I wake up screaming from dreams of kidnapping. I think I'm losing my mind. Maybe I should just cancel."

"You will not cancel your date, Wynter." Jack put his hands on her shoulders and gave her a little shake. "Look at me. He's your dream man. Not only that, you need to relax and let this go. Go out, relax, and get to know this guy." Jack put his finger under her chin, lifting her face and forcing her to meet his gaze.

Wynter frowned. "All right. I'll go out with him."

"That's my girl," Jack said, giving Wynter a hug.

※

Jack watched as Rufus and Wynter padded back to her bedroom. *God, I worry about that girl. She always withdrew into herself, isolating herself from others when she hurt. Damn that stepfather of hers. He really did a number on her. She was so afraid of getting hurt, of being rejected because of her gifts. Now this, a new aspect of her gift, emerging, nightmares of children being kidnapped.*

He hoped things worked out with Wolf. Wynter deserved some happiness in her life. *This Rafe guy better step up to the plate, or he'll have to deal with me.*

8

Wynter looked at her watch and sighed. She only had a few hours before Rafe would be there. She looked around her house. *Not too bad, but it could use a little straightening up*, she thought. Her mind kept drifting back to her date with Rafe. She thought of those oddly colored amber eyes, and she flushed from remembering the heat in them at the bookstore. For a moment, she had thought he was going to kiss her.

God, do I have it bad, she thought. He was handsome, although not handsome in the conventional sense. His face was a bit too rugged to be considered pretty, but still he took her breath away. It was more than his looks that attracted her. He was so supportive and protective of his sister and niece. *Could he really be the one who could accept my gift or rather curse?*

Wynter touched her scarred cheek and remembered her stepfather's reaction. He had called her a demon and beat her mercilessly. Wynter mentally shook herself. She really needed to get it in gear if she wanted to be ready on time.

A warm feeling came over her as she looked around her house, her little nest. She loved color, and it was reflected in her choice of furnishings and paint. Her living room was painted a pale green. The carpet was a deep rose color. An oversize couch the color of hunter green made an L shape with the matching love seat. A rose-colored throw was across the back of the couch.

Wynter picked up the books that were lying on the oak coffee table and placed them upon the matching end table between the couch and love seat. She quickly dusted the flat screen television and ran the duster over the matching bookcases on either side of the television. *Thank goodness I did the heavy cleaning yesterday.*

She hung up a jacket that had fallen on the floor on the coat rack in the foyer. Upstairs were two bedrooms and her studio. The dining room was in good shape, but her office space on the opposite side needed a little tidying. The kitchen was a bright, sunny room with the walls painted a pale yellow, golden oak cabinets, and a huge oak island in the middle of the room. Copper pots hung over the island.

Wynter ran upstairs to take a shower. As she went into her bedroom to get clean underwear, she spied Rufus lying in the middle of the bed. He opened his eyes to look at her and grunted.

Wynter laughed. "I didn't mean to interrupt his majesty's nap."

Rufus grunted again for good measure and went back

to sleep. Grabbing matching bra and panties, Wynter took a long, luxurious shower.

Wrapped in a plush blue towel, Wynter wiped the steam from the mirror and considered the scar running down her cheek, a thin white line that nothing really covered up. *Will Rafe think me ugly?* She needed to have faith that her aunt Helen and her dreams were right, that Rafe could accept and love her.

Wynter carefully applied concealer to minimize her scar. She smoked her eyes with dark blue eye shadow, deepening the color of her eyes. Her features were delicate with eyes that slanted slightly upward, high cheekbones, and pouty lips.

Wynter shook out her hair, deciding to put it up, leaving a few wisps to frame her face. She chose to wear a sapphire-blue short-sleeved 1947 dress. The bodice fit snuggly and then flared into a full sweeping skirt. She slipped on the matching heels and turned to view the end result in the mirror. A small sprite of a woman stared back at her, making her feel like she was playing dress up, as she was more comfortable in jeans and a button-down shirt. Still it was nice to dress up every now and then. She twirled, loving how the skirt flared as she spun around.

She was ready when the doorbell rang. At the sound of the bell, Rufus came flying down the stairs, wagging his tail in anticipation.

"No jumping, Rufus," Wynter said as she grabbed him by the collar and opened the door.

She looked up at Rafe, whose eyes gleamed with sensual promise. "Hi. I mean, come in. Let me get my jacket, and then we can go."

Rufus nudged Rafe's leg. Drool hung from his mouth.

"Hi!" Rafe bent down on one knee and pet Rufus on the head. "Big dog you have here, Wynter."

Wynter smiled. "Don't worry about Rufus. He loves people. Rufus, go lay down now," Wynter commanded.

Rufus swiped his tongue across Rafe's hand and plopped himself down at the foot of the stairway, looking up at Rafe with puppy eyes.

Wynter noticed Rafe's wet hand. "Oh, let me get you a towel. I usually have a towel handy as Rufus can be a bit drooly."

"No, don't worry about it. I don't think he got me." Rafe brushed Rufus's hair from his blue dress shirt and checked his gray slacks for any slobber stains. Rafe's gaze swept over her from head to toe. "You look beautiful."

Wynter blushed. "Thank you." Wynter looked down at her feet. "So do you."

Rafe chuckled. "I've been called many things before, but beautiful is not one of them."

Wynter quickly glanced up at Rafe and then looked away. "Oh, well, I …"

"Hey, sweetheart, it's one of the nicest compliments that I've received from a beautiful woman."

"Oh," Wynter said with a smile.

Rafe glanced around. "You have a lot of books. You could start your own library," he said and smiled.

Wynter slowly looked around the room. "One of my vices. I love to read."

"That's a good thing, right?" Rafe picked up a book and looked at the erotic cover. He smiled. "We should get going."

Wynter put on her jacket and then grabbed her purse. "Okay, I'm all set." She locked the door.

Rafe stepped back and looked at the house. "How old is your house? I love the Victorian style."

Wynter glanced at her home and wondered if she should paint it. Red was such a bold color. She thought the gray shutters complemented the red beautifully. "Well, the main part of the house is over a hundred years old. The later additions, I really don't know how old they are. It's a little quirky, but I love it."

"It's really set back off the road. I almost missed your driveway. Fortunately for me, my sister told me to look for the pink tree," Rafe said.

"Yes, the famous pink tree. The prior owners had the tree painted a shocking hot pink. Good thing too, as I think everyone would miss the driveway," Wynter said with a laugh.

Wynter looked at Rafe's Jeep Cherokee and wondered how she would manage to gracefully get in the SUV. Rafe saw Wynter eyeing the Jeep, and before she could do anything, he came around to the passenger side and lifted Wynter into the Jeep.

"Ah, thanks," Wynter stammered. "It would have been awkward in these heels."

Rafe's hands lingered on Wynter's waist. "My pleasure." Rafe's voice was slightly rough.

Wynter blushed and bit her bottom lip. Wynter felt the heat of attraction as Rafe caressed her scarred cheek. She felt the passion build between them. His hand brushed against her breast. Her breath caught. Trembling, she moved deeper into his embrace. Never had she become aroused so quickly. Her panties were soaked. She felt Rafe's erection nestle against her. A brisk wind stroked its way up her dress. She shivered and pulled back as her panties cooled against her heated skin. *Too soon. It's too soon.*

A blush stained her cheeks. She placed her hands on his chest and gave a little push. "Ummm, where are we going?" Wynter asked in a rush.

Rafe took a deep breath and stepped back. "I ..." Rafe cleared his throat. "I thought we would try out the new chef at my brother-in-law's place."

She took a deep breath. "Oh, I love Second Chances. They have wonderful food."

It was a short drive to the restaurant. The hostess led them to a table in the corner with a view of the lake. "Wow, you must really rate. This is a wonderful view of the lake."

The restaurant was elegant and cozy at the same time. Pink tablecloths covered the tables. The lighting was dim, and each table had a glowing lantern. The ceiling had dark mahogany wood beams, giving the place some character. A waiter came and took their drink order.

Though Rafe invaded her dreams, Wynter realized she really knew nothing about him. She leaned back in her chair. "So I hear you are joining old man Jeffrey's law firm."

Rafe frowned. "Yes, I guess news travels fast."

Wynter smiled. "You have to love small towns. Best grapevines in the world. My cousin Jack told me. I hope you don't mind."

Rafe drummed his fingers. "I guess it will take some

adjustment." He reached for Wynter's hand. "Thankfully I have nothing to hide. I guess turnabout is fair play. My sister told me that you're an artist."

Wynter rubbed her scar and chuckled. "Yes, I guess you can say I'm an artist."

Rafe smiled and rubbed the back of her hand. "What does that mean? Hmmm. Now that I think about it, there are many different types of art. What kind of artist are you?"

"I do illustrations for children's books, and I design covers for romance novels. Not very glamorous, but it pays the bills."

"And in your spare time you find missing children?" Rafe asked.

Wynter had taken a sip of water and swallowed wrong, causing her to choke and cough.

"Are you all right?" Rafe asked as he half rose from his seat.

Wynter held up her hand, indicating to give her a moment, and nodded her head. Taking a deep breath, she was finally able to take a breath without coughing.

Rafe resumed his seat and took a deep breath. "I didn't mean to upset you. I know you helped to find Iris, and I thought I heard Special Agent Steele say something about you being psychic."

Wynter dabbed at her watering eyes with her napkin. She looked at Rafe and sighed, twirling a loose curl around her finger. She thought she might have had a little more time before having this conversation. "Psychic. I guess that is as good as any word to describe it. Sometimes

I know things before they happen. But mainly I find things, sometimes people."

Rafe looked like he was about to say something, and Wynter held up her hand. "No, I really don't know how it works or why I get …" Wynter hesitated. "Visions, for want of a better word, it just happens." Her voice was husky and vulnerable.

Wynter ran her finger down her scar. "If you lose something and you have a connection to it, like your keys, a … I don't know … a picture will form within my mind, showing me where they are."

Rafe frowned. "I take it that people don't respond well when you tell them you're psychic."

Wynter's eyes became unfocused as she remembered her stepfather and his reaction to her visions. "No, people don't take it well. They think I'm some kind of freak. I've learned not to advertise that I'm a finder. It's safer that way." Wynter's hand shook as she picked up her wine and took a sip.

Rafe looked sharply at Wynter and noticed her hand tremble. "It's a lot to take in, but if it were a vision that helped you find Iris, then I have to say that I am grateful that you have visions." Rafe reached for Wynter's hand. "So delicate." He ran his thumb across her hand. "Why don't we talk about something else for now and enjoy our dinner?" Rafe asked with a forced smile.

Wynter felt some of the tension leave her as she realized that Rafe wasn't going to call her a demon's spawn or worse. A sigh of relief escaped.

"Yes, I think that's a splendid idea."

On the drive home, Rafe thought about the conflicting emotions that Wynter stirred up inside of him. He couldn't believe how quickly he became aroused when he was around her. *Hell, just thinking about her gives me a hard-on.* But it wasn't just a physical reaction. She got under his skin. When he saw how fearful she got when she spoke of her gift, it brought out all his protective instincts.

Rafe sighed. He really wasn't up to dealing with her visions. *Of course she has visions. How ironic*, Rafe thought.

This past year he had so much to deal with: George's gambling and theft problems and then his ex Gina with her crazy superstitions ruling her life. He didn't have time to deal with someone else's visions and dreams right now, no matter how many times Wynter had invaded his. He just couldn't go there.

9

WYNTER BLINKED AS SHE stared at Daisy's blonde dyed hair, which now sported pink streaks.

"Morning, honey. You waiting on Jack?" Daisy asked with a gleam in her eye.

Wynter looked down at the menu in her hand. "Like the new hair color, Daisy."

"Thanks, sweetie. What can I get ya?" Daisy asked with a wink.

"Ummm, I'll have an Earl Grey tea with honey and an everything bagel with cream cheese." Wynter looked up at Daisy and smiled. "And yes, I'm meeting Jack. I'm sure he'll want his usual."

"You got it, sugar." Daisy then went to wait on another customer.

Jack walked in and looked handsome in his usual sheriff's uniform of blue button-down shirt, jeans, and cowboy boots. He wore his shoulder holster and badge well.

"Thanks for saving my seat," he said as he slid into his favorite booth, placing his hat next to him.

"I placed your usual order with Daisy."

"Good, good. So how was last night?" Jack asked and smiled.

"Hey, sugar, I got your usual right here. How you doin', sweetie?" Daisy winked at Wynter.

Jack glanced at Daisy with his gaze fixed on her hair. "Nice color, Daisy. The pink is a good touch."

Daisy patted her hair and gave Jack a big smile. "Thanks, I'm glad you like it." Daisy winked at Jack and sashayed to her next table.

Jack chuckled. "Pink hair. What's next?" Jack took a sip of his coffee and then turned his attention to his food. "Details, girl. Give me details."

Wynter nibbled at her bagel and then took a sip of her tea. "I guess it went well."

Jack looked up with fork suspended in midair. "You guess! What kind of answer is that? Either you had a good time or you didn't."

Wynter fingered her scar and shrugged. "It started out well. Then he brought up my gift, and well, I don't know."

"I'm guessing he didn't take it well."

Wynter looked up at Jack and shrugged again. "It's not that. I mean …" Wynter took a deep breath. "He just kind of gave me a weird vibe, if you know what I mean. We ended up changing the subject. I mean we talked for hours, about … well … movies we liked, work, and books."

Wynter looked down at her lap and blushed. "But he didn't kiss me good night." She glanced at Jack. "I mean, at first I thought he really seemed attracted to me. There was a moment in his truck," Wynter stammered.

"Anyway, he just seemed to pull back after I told him about my gift." Wynter ran her finger down her scar. "Maybe I shouldn't have said visions because that's not really how it works. Or maybe it does. You hand me something of the missing person, and I get a vision of where they might be, so yeah, I guess vision works."

"Aw, honey, did he ask you out again?" Jack took a sip of his coffee.

Wynter shook her head. In a restless move, she rolled up the sleeves of her oversized white button-down shirt. "No, we kind of left it up in the air. That's bad, right?"

"It's not good," Jack said. "Maybe he needs some time to wrap his mind around what you can do. I mean, it's not every day that you meet someone who finds kids and other things."

"Maybe." Wynter sighed. "What should I do?"

"Give him a few days. Then give him a call or something."

Wynter sighed. "I guess I can do that."

The bell rang over the door, and in walked Sandy McBride, who looked pretty in her black floral print faux wrap swing dress, along with her two sons, eight-year-old Jeff and ten-year-old Tommy, both dressed in jeans and sweatshirts.

Jack looked over and pushed away his plate. He sat back in his seat and sighed. Wynter looked up and noticed Jack looking longingly at Sandy, who was of average height and had light red hair and a sprinkle of freckles across her face.

"When are you going to ask her out, Jack? You've been mooning over her since she came back into town."

Jack looked back at his cousin. "You know how hurt she was when Sam took off with all their money, leaving her alone to raise their two sons."

Wynter picked up her mug of tea. "It's been two years now. They've been divorced for over a year. I think Sandy would appreciate a night out. She's always had a thing for you. You two would make a great couple. I'm glad she moved back home."

Jack looked back over at Sandy and sighed again. "I don't know. Are you sure it's not too soon?"

Wynter threw her napkin at Jack. "No, it's not too soon. Hey, I'm gonna call Rafe. I think you can get the courage to ask Sandy for a date."

"You know I struck out with her back in high school. What makes you think she'll go out with me now?" Jack scratched the side of his nose.

Wynter huffed. "In high school, you were some big jock who had all these cheerleaders falling all over themselves to get close to you. And that bitch Kimberly said some nasty things to Sandy. You know Kimberly always thought she owned you." Wynter leaned back in her seat. "Now you're the sheriff, and you've grown up some. I see how she looks at you when you're not looking. I think she likes you and would jump at the chance to go out with you."

Jack smiled. "You would think that. Maybe you're right and I should ask her out."

"Of course I'm right." Wynter smirked.

Rafe woke up and sniffed appreciatively. He rolled out of bed, putting on sweats and a T-shirt. He ambled into the kitchen and yawned.

"Good morning," he said as he walked into the kitchen, got a mug from the cabinet above the coffeepot, and poured himself a cup. He took a deep appreciative breath before he took his first sip of coffee.

Gabby turned and kissed Rafe on the cheek. "Morning, sleepyhead. I'm making waffles for breakfast. You want some?"

"Sure, that would be great. I haven't had a good homemade breakfast in a while."

Gabby glanced at her brother as she poured the batter into the griddle. "So how was your date last night with Wynter?"

Rafe took another sip of his coffee. "Fine. Where are John and Iris?" He leaned back against the counter.

"John had to go in early for deliveries, and Iris is still in bed." Gabby tapped the baby monitor. "What does fine mean? Fine tells me nothing."

Rafe frowned and put his mug down on the counter. "Look, I think Wynter is really nice, but I don't know if I want to get involved with a woman …" Rafe used air quotes. "Who gets visions. You know the mess I went through with Gina with all that magic mumbo-jumbo crap. I just can't go through that again."

Gabby quickly looked up from the griddle. "Visions! I never heard that Wynter had visions. I mean, she's so down to earth, so grounded. Are you sure you heard that right?"

Rafe shrugged. "Yeah, I'm sure. She told me about them last night."

"What kind of visions are we talking about here?" Gabby put a plate of waffles on the table.

Rafe rolled his eyes, grabbed his mug, and sat down at the kitchen table. "Look, Wynter told me that she doesn't advertise it, so keep this between us. I don't think I should say anything else about it. It seemed that she had some bad experiences with people who found out that she has visions. Just don't say anything, okay?"

"Okay, I won't say anything. Whatever." Gabby frowned and rubbed her forehead. "Are you sure this is about Gina and not about—"

Rafe slammed down his mug. "No, it's not about him!" He glared at Gabby. He was not going to talk about his grandfather.

"Oookay! You know, Rafe, anyone can see that Wynter is nothing like Gina. You're attracted to her, right?" Gabby sat down next to Rafe and took a sip of her coffee.

Rafe rubbed the side of his nose. "Well yeah, I'm attracted to her, but—"

Gabby glared at Rafe and interrupted, "No buts, Rafe. Don't let one bad experience with Gina cloud your judgment about Wynter. She's the first woman you've shown an interest in, in like forever. Also, she makes Iris laugh. Gina hated spending time with Iris. All I'm saying is to get to know her before you make any decisions."

Rafe narrowed his eyes. "We'll see," he finally said.

※

Wynter got into her VW Bug and turned the key in the ignition. Nothing happened. She turned the key again and still nothing. *Damn, just what I need*, Wynter thought. She got out of the car and went back into the house to call Roger Thorpe, the local mechanic. She ran her finger down her scar as she waited for Roger to answer the phone.

"Hey, Roger. It's Wynter Malone. My car won't start. I don't know if it's my battery or not. Could you come out and check it out? Good. See you in a bit," Wynter said and then disconnected the call.

She rubbed Rufus's head. "Looks like it's going to be one of those days. Come on, boy. Let's go back in the house and wait for Roger." Wynter looked at the clouds and wrapped her arms around herself. "I guess I'll be working from home today."

※

Walter Jeffrey was a portly man in his late sixties with warm brown eyes and gray hair. He was relaxed sitting behind a beautiful mahogany desk. There was an orderly air to his office with law books filling the bookcase on one side of the room and a window on the other side.

He looked at Rafe and smiled. "I think that's everything. I left the files that are active in the conference room. I talked to all the clients, letting them know that you will be joining the firm and will be handling their cases while I am on vacation. I know it's not what you're used to, but it'll keep you busy. We'll meet with the clients before I leave. This is gonna be a big change for you. Are you sure you're up for small-town lawyering?"

Rafe smiled. "You have no idea. But it's not like I don't have experience with a general law practice. I interned for a firm that was diversified in its practice."

"I'm glad you're here. My wife and I are looking forward to spending some time with my daughter and her family. Don't worry. Sandy is a great paralegal, and she will be a great help to you while I'm gone." Walter leaned back in his chair.

"I was impressed with her when we spoke yesterday. I'll need all the help I can get while I acclimate to a more diverse practice," Rafe said as he loosened his tie.

Walter chuckled. "You'll have no problems. Sandy will steer you right." He stood up and grabbed his jacket.

"You're going to Florida, right?" Rafe stood up as well.

"Yep, it'll be great to see my grandkids. I hope to retire in a couple of years, and Florida is looking like a great place for it. I'm glad you're here, Rafe. This way the clients will get to know you before I retire. If any problems come up while I'm away, you have my cell phone number. Give me a call if you have any questions," Walter said.

Rafe clapped Walter on his back. "I'm glad to be here. I think I'll enjoy the diversity of the work."

※

A couple of hours later, Rafe stood up and stretched. He'd reviewed the open cases and talked with Sandy. This was certainly different from corporate law. Hopefully it wouldn't take long for him to adjust. *Sandy will be a lifesaver*, Rafe thought.

It was time to quit for the day. Rafe drove to his sister's and thought about Wynter. *God, I wanted to kiss her last night. Hell, I wanted to do a lot more than that. What is it with this damn attraction?* She kept invading his thoughts and dreams. *Maybe Gabby was right. Maybe I should give this, whatever this is, a chance.*

Sheriff Johnson seemed to think she had some sort of gift. She did help find Iris. *Yeah*, he thought, *I'll give her a call*.

※

Wynter was curled up in her favorite spot on the couch, sipping a cup of tea and petting Rufus who was half lying on her lap. *God, I hope it doesn't take Roger long to fix my Bug. Now I have to reschedule my meeting with my agent*, Wynter thought.

She snuggled deeper into the couch and looked at Rufus. "Maybe the dreams are wrong, Rufus. Maybe Rafe isn't the one. I know Aunt Helen thinks otherwise. I just don't know what to think." Wynter gave Rufus a hug. "No point in worrying about it. Only time will tell if Rafe is the one. Come on, boy. You need to go out. Then it's off to bed."

※

Blackness enveloped her sight. She fought and pushed against the suffocating dark. She gulped in air, trying to catch her breath. She opened her eyes and squinted. In the distance, she could see a light. Taking a deep breath, she pushed against the dark as she stumbled toward the light. The light revealed a window. She walked slowly toward it. A puff of air escaped as she grasped. She leaned toward the warmth of the light and shivered. She saw a boy in a chair. She squinted again as she tried to peer through the window. Shadows danced around. In between shafts of light, she could make out a form. It looked ... yes, it was a child. A familiar coldness seeped deep in her bones. I felt this way before, she thought as she watched the boy struggle in this chair. A scream pierced the shadows.

Wynter woke with a start, soaked in sweat. *Damn, another dream. No point in calling Jack.* There was nothing new to tell him, just a vague impression of the scary kidnapper and a feeling of danger. She had a feeling that, whatever was going to happen, he would be the catalyst for the disaster she could sense was about to happen. It was odd, but she felt some kind of connection to this man. And well, that was just ridiculous.

There was no point in trying to go back to sleep. She glanced at the clock on the nightstand. It read 3:30 a.m. She threw off the covers and got out of bed. She padded downstairs into the living room. *Maybe a little TV will help me relax.*

Rufus stretched, jumped off the bed, and followed Wynter downstairs. Wynter curled up in her favorite chair in the living room with the TV on low. Rufus was comfortable, sprawled out on the couch. How she missed her mother at times like this. She missed being able to talk to her about her dreams of Rafe. Now she had this other thing to contend with, dreams of kidnapping. She always focused better after speaking with her mother.

Aunt Helen was wonderful, and she knew she could talk to her, but her dreams about Rafe were so intimate, so erotic. Just thinking about them made her blush. She was sure she would have been more comfortable talking with her mother. *But then again, maybe not.*

Wynter frowned down into her cup of tea. What she never understood was why her mother married her stepfather. Neil Malone was no Prince Charming, at least not with her. Even though he adopted her and she bore his surname, their relationship had always been difficult. She could never bring herself to think of him as her father.

A small smile flittered across her face as she remembered how her mother would hide things for her to find and how she helped her build her shields to prevent her from being overwhelmed by lost items and the people who lost them whenever she touched something.

God! How I miss my mom.

Aunt Helen took over teaching her, but it just wasn't the same.

I miss you so much, Mom, she thought.

※

A handsome, silver-haired man reclined back in his chair and took a sip of whisky as he gazed at the big man who sat across from him. "Oscar is becoming a problem. He's not playing by the rules or following orders. If he is allowed to continue down this path, he'll lead the feds right to our door. That is unacceptable. Find out what he's up to," he commanded.

The big man smiled, and the light gleamed off his shaved head. "It'll be my pleasure, boss."

❦

Wynter was sitting on her back porch, wrapped in a quilt, watching the sun rise. A serene smile was on her face when she felt the presence of another.

"Morning, Jack."

"Morning, cuz. You got any coffee?"

"Knew you were coming. It should be finished brewing right about now."

Jack went into the kitchen, poured himself a cup of coffee, returned to the porch, and sat next to Wynter. He gave her a quick look and frowned. "You look like hell, kiddo."

Wynter stuck out her tongue and smacked Jack on the arm. "What every woman wants to hear."

Jack put his hand on her shoulder and gave it a gentle squeeze. "Rough night?"

"Bad dreams." Wynter sighed.

"Thought as much. You know I'm here for you?" Jack said as he gazed at the lake.

Wynter smiled as she sipped her tea. "I know. What else might bring my handsome cousin out to see me?"

Jack coughed. "Well, I thought maybe you could do a favor for me. I lost—"

"Special Agent Steele's phone number." Wynter closed

her eyes and saw Steele's business card in the top drawer of Jack's dresser. "Top dresser drawer."

Jack stretched out his long legs. "Thanks, cuz."

"Anytime, brother of my heart."

"It's amazing how you do that."

"Yeah, amazing." Wynter snorted.

10

John leaned in the doorway, watching as Gabby seasoned steaks. He gazed warmly as he took in her disheveled hair. "Are you sure you don't want me to help with dinner?" John asked.

Gabby gave John a tight smile. "No, you cook all the time at the restaurant. I know you're picking up the slack for me. I'm just not ready ... I have to keep watch ... I know. I know. I have to stop, but I ... not right now." Gabby flushed and looked away from John. "I want you to be able to relax while you're home."

John came up behind Gabby and kissed her neck. "I don't mind, you know? I love cooking for you." John looked at the steaks. "Five steaks. Isn't that a bit much for three adults and one kid? I know Rafe has a hearty appetite, but even he won't eat two steaks."

Gabby stepped away from John and washed her hands. "I invited Wynter to have dinner with us."

"Is that wise? I think Rafe can handle his own love life." John pulled a beer from the refrigerator.

Gabby dried her hands. "Wynter is the first woman that Rafe has shown any interest in since Gina. I like her, and she's good with Iris. He just needs a push in the right direction." Gabby walked over to John and punched him in the arm. "And how come you never told me that Wynter has visions? I mean, I've heard some vague rumors about Wynter's family, but you've lived here all your life. What's up with Wynter and her family?"

John frowned and took a swig of his beer. "They're a very private family. I went to school with Jack, but we didn't hang out together." John sat down at the kitchen table and relaxed back in the chair. "There have always been rumors about Wynter's family. It seems that the women in her family often have …"

John shrugged. "I don't know. Things they could do. Like Wynter's aunt is good with herbs and growing things. People go to her for remedies. As for Wynter, she didn't grow up here. When her mother married her stepfather, they moved away. It wasn't until Wynter was about eleven or twelve that she moved in with the Johnsons. She's younger than I am, so I didn't really have much contact with her. From what I did see of her, well, she was always quiet, a little on the shy side." John looked at Gabby. "I never heard anything about Wynter having visions. Where did you hear about it?"

Gabby blushed and covered her mouth with her hand. "Oh no! Rafe said Wynter doesn't advertise that she has visions. I shouldn't have said anything." Gabby twisted her hands together. "Promise me you won't say anything,

John. I like Wynter, and I don't want to do anything to hurt her," Gabby pleaded.

John grabbed Gabby and pulled her onto his lap. "Hey, what's this about?" He wiped away her tears.

Gabby hiccupped. "She's been so nice to me since …" Gabby drifted off. "And well, I don't have many friends here." Gabby shook her head. "I don't know why I'm so upset. It's just that Wynter doesn't treat me like I'm fragile and gonna break."

John kissed Gabby on her nose. "I promise I won't say anything. Wynter's secret is safe with me."

Rafe walked into the kitchen. "Hey, guys." He took in Gabby sitting on John's lap and smiled. "I'm gonna go take a shower and leave you two lovebirds alone."

※

After his shower, feeling more relaxed, Rafe walked into the kitchen to grab a beer and cast an appreciative look at his sister's fancy green blouse and designer jeans. "Hey, sis, don't you look nice?" he said as he kissed his sister's cheek.

Gabby blushed. "Thanks, Rafe."

"Anything I can help you with?" Rafe took a sip of his beer.

Gabby smiled at Rafe. "No, everything is under control."

Rafe leaned against the counter and crossed his jean-clad legs. "I've been meaning to talk to you. If you and John want to get away for an evening or even a weekend, I'd be happy to watch Iris."

Gabby stiffened and looked at her brother. "I don't know—"

Rafe interrupted, "Come on, Gabby. I know Iris being taken last year was horrible, but you can't monitor her twenty-four seven. It's not healthy for Iris, and it's not healthy for you or your marriage." Rafe put his beer down on the counter and grabbed Gabby in a fierce hug. "I'm not saying you have to rush into anything. I do think you should take some baby steps and let me watch Iris one night while you and John go out for dinner or something. I'm worried about you, kiddo."

Gabby looked up at her brother and shrugged. "I know. I know. My therapist says the same thing. It's not as easy as you think. I panic when I don't know where Iris is. I mean, what if she's taken again? I couldn't bear it."

Rafe wiped a tear from Gabby's cheek. "Aw, honey. The world is a dangerous place, but keeping tabs on Iris twenty-four seven isn't going to do Iris any favors. She'll learn to be afraid to take risks. You and John need alone time too. Just think about it. Maybe you bake something here and drive it over to the restaurant. Baby steps, Gabby. Baby steps."

"I know you're right. I'll try." Gabby gave a sigh of relief when the doorbell rang. A mischievous light lit her eyes. "I'll get it," she said as she hurried out of the kitchen.

Dressed comfortably in worn jeans and green sweater, John walked in the kitchen. He grabbed a beer from the refrigerator, twisted off the cap, and took a sip.

"Hey, John. I didn't know you were expecting company," Rafe said.

John laughed. "I see Gabby didn't tell you."

"Tell me what?"

"Wynter, can I get you a glass of wine?" Gabby asked as she walked into the kitchen with Wynter following behind her.

"That would be lovely." Wynter smiled shyly at Rafe. "Hi, Rafe." Then she looked toward John. "Hi, John."

"How's it going?" John asked.

"Good. Busy," Wynter said.

Rafe gave his sister a hard look and then turned to Wynter. "Good to see you, Wynter."

Gabby pushed her hair back and gave Rafe a nervous glance. "Dinner will be ready in a few minutes. John, will you check on the steaks?" Gabby handed Wynter a glass of pinot noir.

"Thank you, Gabby." Wynter took a sip of her wine. "Ummm, it's good, Gabby."

"Why don't you and Rafe go into the dining room? John and I will be in shortly," Gabby said, giving Wynter a wink.

Wynter looked up at Rafe and saw his hard expression. "I guess you didn't know I was coming to dinner." Wynter fingered her scar as they walked into the dining room.

Rafe blew out a breath. *Okay, so I didn't know Wynter was coming for dinner tonight, but this could work out to my advantage. I was going to call her anyway*, he thought. Rafe let his gaze drift over Wynter. She was dressed in a soft white, long-sleeved shirt and dress jeans.

"You look lovely," Rafe said and felt a rush of desire. Never had he felt such a strong physical response to a woman. It was driving him crazy.

Yeah, I'm glad she came, he thought.

Wynter's breath caught, and she blushed furiously. "Thank … thank you," she said breathlessly.

※

"Mmmm, this tiramisu is delicious, Gabby." Wynter pushed her plate back, relaxed deeper into her chair, and took a sip of tea. "Dinner was wonderful. Thank you again for inviting me."

Gabby blushed. "I'm glad you enjoyed it."

"Gabby has always made fantastic desserts." John winked at Gabby.

Wynter glanced at Rafe and flushed a pale pink. The looks he'd been giving her all night made her toes curl. She felt overheated and excited. His eyes glowed like hot amber and brought forth images of them entwined together. Her dreams were exploding into reality.

Gabby coughed, bringing Wynter back to the present. Wynter glanced at her watch and sighed. "I should be going. I have a busy day tomorrow. I really hate to eat and run, but I have some deadlines that I need to meet."

"Let me get your jacket," John said.

"Thanks." Wynter stood up and looked at Gabby. "Maybe you and John would come over to my place on Saturday. Jack and Sandy are coming over, and it should be fun."

Gabby shook her head.

"Bring Iris. Sandy is bringing her boys. It'll be fun. Iris could help me give the boys pointers on drawing."

Gabby gave Wynter a shy smile. "Yes, that would be great. Iris really loves your studio."

"Hey, am I invited to this shindig?" Rafe asked, giving Wynter a wink.

"Well … yes, of course you're invited, I mean …" Wynter's voice trailed off as she lost herself in his gaze.

"Rafe," Gabby said, throwing her napkin at him, "stop teasing Wynter."

Wynter shook her head, trying to clear her thoughts.

"Here's your jacket, Wynter. This was really fun. We should do this again," John said as he handed Wynter her leather jacket.

Wynter put on her jacket. "Gabby, dinner was lovely. Thank you for inviting me."

Gabby hugged Wynter. "I'm so glad you came. I guess I'll see you tomorrow. I am just amazed at some of the drawings that Iris brings home with her."

"She's got a lot of natural talent. I'll see you tomorrow," Wynter said, smiling.

Rafe took Wynter's hand. "I'll see you out." Rafe opened the door and turned on the outside light. "Where's your car?"

"I had to take it in for repairs. Jack dropped me off on his way home from work."

"Is he picking you up?"

"Ah, no. My aunt's house isn't that far from here, so I thought I would just walk to her house and ask my uncle to drive me home."

Rafe glared at Wynter. "What!"

"I, ummm, I'll walk to my aunt's house?" Wynter said with a shrug.

Rafe made a quick decision. "I'm taking you home."

Wynter shook her head. "Really, it's not that far to my aunt's."

Rafe turned to face her. "I am taking you home. No arguments."

Wynter stifled a smile. "Bossy much?" she said playfully.

Rafe tugged on a curl. "Protective. There's a difference. Besides, what kind of gentleman would I be if I allowed a lady to walk to her aunt's house in the dark?"

Wynter smiled. "Well, when you put it like that, you leave me no choice but to accept."

"It isn't just that. Bad things do happen in small towns, you know."

"Oh, Rafe, I'm sorry. I didn't mean to bring back bad memories."

Rafe smiled. "Not a problem. Just want to make sure you get home safe." Rafe yelled back to the kitchen, "I'm taking Wynter home." He smiled at Wynter, took a camel hair coat from the closet, and put it on. "After you, my lady," Rafe said as he opened the door.

Wynter shivered as the crisp night air hit her in the face. "I really appreciate this."

"My pleasure."

Rafe couldn't believe how his body responded to Wynter's presence. His whole body tightened with awareness. She had the most kissable mouth he'd ever seen.

"Here, let me get the car door for you," Rafe said.

Wynter climbed into Rafe's SUV and scooted closer to the driver's side as Rafe closed the door for her. Rafe walked in front of the SUV and then climbed in next to

Wynter. When he started the car, a cold blast of air hit them.

"It'll take a minute for the car to warm up," Rafe said.

"Thanks again for driving me home. It would have been a cold walk to my aunt's," Wynter said and shivered.

Rafe watched Wynter lick her lips, and his thoughts scattered. "Ah, no problem."

A short drive later, Rafe pulled in front of Wynter's house and turned off the engine.

Wynter glanced up at Rafe and took a deep breath. "You want to come in for a nightcap?"

Rafe's gaze heated. "Yes, I'd like that."

"Come on in then. I need to let Rufus out. I have brandy in the pantry. It's on the top shelf. If you wouldn't mind pouring our drinks, I'll just be a few minutes with Rufus?"

"Sounds good." Rafe went into the kitchen and found the brandy on the top shelf of the pantry. He opened the cabinet next to the pantry and found two brandy snifters. He poured the brandy and took it into the living room, setting them down on the coffee table while he waited for Wynter.

Rufus rushed in and bumped his massive head against Rafe's leg, begging to be pet.

"Rufus, give Rafe some space, buddy."

"He's very friendly," Rafe said as he rubbed Rufus's floppy ear.

"Jack would take him to the station with him when he was a puppy, so he got a lot of socialization when he was young. He can be very possessive, and socializing him helped keep that in check."

"You and Jack seem close."

Wynter nodded. "Jack and Sara are my best friends as well as my cousins. They made a place for me within their family."

"Sara?"

"Jack's sister. We're the same age, and she took me under her wing, introducing me to her friends and …" Wynter sighed. "And generally she made school easier for me."

"John told me a little about your move to Black Falls. I'm guessing that Sara doesn't live around here, as no one has mentioned her."

Wynter nodded. "No, she lives outside of the DC area," she said as she sat down. "Come, sit down." Wynter swirled her brandy. "I'm glad you're not upset that Gabby invited me to dinner tonight."

Rafe sat down next to Wynter on the couch. He reached out and pulled on one of her curls, amazed how it sprung back into shape. "I'm really glad you came."

Wynter took a sip of brandy. "Really? Because I kind of felt like you weren't really interested in seeing me again."

Rafe put down his glass and took her hand in his. "I admit, when you told me about your visions, I kind of freaked. My last girlfriend was into tarot cards, fortune-tellers, and all that superstition junk. I mean, she couldn't make a decision without first consulting her fortune-teller. So when you told me you had visions, well, it gave me a flashback, and I panicked. I know that your gift is nothing like Gina's beliefs. I kind of overreacted."

A mischievous light entered Wynter's eyes. "Yes, I'll

say. Everyone knows tea leaves are the best for getting answers to questions."

Rafe choked on his brandy. "What?"

Wynter laughed. "I'm joking."

Rafe wiped his mouth. "Good to know."

Wynter wiped her eye as she chuckled. "You should have seen your face," she said as she placed her glass on the coffee table.

Rafe tugged her curls again. "That's a twisted sense of humor you have there."

Wynter smiled. "So I've been told."

Rafe placed his empty glass next to Wynter's. "You know, there's something I've been wanting to do all night," he said as he tugged her into his embrace. His mouth came down upon hers.

Her lips opened beneath his. Her sweet response sent him over the edge. His hand cupped her breast. She moaned in pleasure and wrapped her arms around his neck.

"I've dreamed of this," Rafe murmured against her lips. "You have no idea how much I want you."

"Rafe." Wynter sighed.

He couldn't believe the explosion of passion he felt. He could feel the connection between them, strengthening in ways he didn't want to think about. Rafe scooped her up in his arms.

"Where?" Rafe moaned. He could drown in her gaze. Her eyes seemed to glow with her desire.

"Upstairs, first door on the left," she whispered, clutching at his neck.

Rafe scooped Wynter up into his arms and went up

the stairs. He kicked open the door to Wynter's bedroom and entered the bedroom, taking in the queen-size bed that faced a big bay window and french doors that led to a balcony. He gently laid her upon the bed, kissing her neck as he slowly unbuttoned her shirt, revealing a delicate white lace bra.

Wynter pushed up Rafe's sweater and ran her hands over his chest. Rafe took over and pulled off his sweater, hungry for Wynter's touch. He took off her bra and cupped one of her breasts into his palm.

"Beautiful," he breathed. He bent his head and took her nipple into his mouth, gently sucking it.

Wynter unbuttoned his jeans. "A little help here. Off, jeans. Off."

Rafe took off his boots and quickly shed his jeans. He leaned over Wynter, unbuttoned her jeans, and pulled them off, leaving her in her white lace panties.

Wynter ran her thumbs under the waistband of her panties and started to slowly push them down. Rafe pushed down his own undershorts, freeing his erection. He leaned over Wynter and skimmed his hand down her body until he reached her soft core and slipped his fingers into her wet heat and groaned. Wynter made a low hungry sound that jacked up all his senses with pleasure pulsing through him.

Wynter grabbed his hand and pressed it against her wet heat. "Please, Rafe, now."

"In a minute, baby," he said as his fingers stroked her passions higher.

"Rafe, I can't." Wynter moaned.

"Hush, baby. Just let go."

Wynter's eyes fluttered shut as the climax exploded, taking her breath. She let out a breathless sigh and floated on clouds of pleasures. "That's it, baby."

Rafe fumbled for his jeans, which he had thrown on the floor. He grabbed a condom from the back pocket of his jeans, tore the foil packet, and rolled the condom onto his erection.

Rafe slowly entered her, stretching her. *God, she is so tight.* Sweat gleamed on his body as he fought for control. Wynter thrust her hips up, taking more of him.

"Rafe," she whispered.

Rafe drove deep within her, gasping in pleasure. With every thrust, he felt the pleasure build and roared as he ejaculated.

Wynter clenched her legs around his waist and shuddered, as she once again was thrown into orgasm. Electricity sparked between them as they found their release.

Rafe collapsed upon her and panted. "God, that was intense! I've never experienced anything like it." Gently he rolled off Wynter, taking her with him, so her head rested upon his shoulder.

Wynter blew the hair from her eyes. "Wow. Just wow."

Rafe chuckled. 'Yeah, wow."

11

Rafe woke with Wynter snuggled in his arms. He ran his hand down her back and felt raised lines marring her skin. He lowered the sheet and was stunned by the vivid dragon that graced her back, done in bold greens, blues, gold, and pink. When he looked closer, he could see the scars that the dragon covered. *What the hell*, he thought.

Wynter snuggled deeper into the covers. "I told you people don't often take kindly to my gift. My stepfather certainly didn't," Wynter whispered against his chest.

"I'm sorry," Rafe said as he traced the dragon. "I had no idea. I mean John told me your stepfather abused you and that was why you went to live with the Johnsons, but—"

Wynter put her finger over Rafe's lips. "Not many know the details. It happened a long time ago." Wynter reached up to place a soft kiss upon Rafe's lips. "It's one of the reasons I don't tell many people about my gift."

"I didn't know," Rafe said as he kissed her forehead. A cold rage filled him. "Where's your stepfather now?"

"He died a few years back," Wynter said with a shrug and snuggled once again against his chest.

Rafe jumped as he felt something cold and wet touch his foot. His cold anger dissolved. "Jeez, what the hell is that?"

Wynter giggled. "I think Rufus likes you."

Rafe looked at the end of the bed and saw Rufus with his tongue hanging out.

"He's the best alarm clock ever," Wynter quipped.

※

The sun shone brightly on Saturday, making the day unseasonably warm. Wynter sat on the blanket with her legs stretched out before her as she leaned against a tree and watched Rafe playing with Rufus. She smiled, truly believing for the first time that maybe there was something to those dreams that the women of her family had of their destined mates, the Rose Legacy. She waved him over when he glanced her way. Rufus ran over to Wynter, dropping his slobbered-on ball in her lap.

"Thanks, buddy," Wynter said as she picked the ball up with her thumb and forefinger, trying not to transfer the slobber onto herself. Wynter looked up at Rafe and smiled. "We told Sandy we'd meet her at her house around ten. We need to get going if we're going to make it on time."

"It shouldn't take us too long to pick up the folding tables and chairs," Rafe said.

"I can't believe how quickly this gathering has grown from just having Jack and Sandy to including the kids, your sister's family, friends of Jack's, and my family."

"I'm looking forward to tonight. It'll be wonderful. Just wait and see," Rafe said, smiling.

Wynter scratched her head. "This barbeque thing really took off. I didn't realize how many people I'd invited. I've never had so many people over at one time. I'm kind of nervous, if the truth be known. Thank God for Sandy. Otherwise these people wouldn't have a place to sit and eat."

※

The day was cool and vibrant. Jack, Rafe, John, Hank, and Stuart, all dressed casually in jeans and sweaters, stood around the grill, waiting for the hamburgers and hot dogs to cook.

"It's beautiful here in the fall," Rafe said.

"Yeah, Wynter was lucky when she bought this place. It was advertised as a handyman special, and you know who got roped into being the handyman," Jack said, chuckling. "The repairs weren't too bad."

"I love the pond. Take a boat out there during the summer, relaxing in the sun and catching fish," John said, smiling. "Yeah, that's the life."

"Yeah, instead of repairing the roof, the prior owners put in this pond. It's really beautiful, but I never understood how they could let the house go the way they did," Stuart said.

Laughter wafted toward them from where the ladies

sat while watching the kids play with Rufus, who was pulling them like a train around the yard. Wynter looked at Daisy's purple streaks that matched the sweater she was wearing.

"I'm so glad you and Hank were able to come. Who's minding the diner?" Wynter asked.

"My sister Peggy and her son Chip. They are in seventh heaven, especially Chip who will be handling the kitchen on his own today," Daisy said with a laugh.

Daisy gave Sandy a sly look. "It's good to see you out and about with your boys. Jack is looking mighty fine today, wouldn't you say?" she said with a wink.

Sandy blushed. "Jack always looks good. I mean, yes. Yes, he does."

"You're working with Gabby's brother. How's that going?" Daisy asked.

"Rafe's great. It's fun showing him the ropes of the office. He's still getting acquainted with a small-town practice. He has a little trouble with clients oversharing about their lives, if you know what I mean," Sandy said with a laugh.

"When do the Jeffreys get back from Florida? I'm sure things will settle into a rhythm once Walter is back in the office," Gabby said.

"They are enjoying Florida and their grandkids. They should be back later this month."

Daisy smiled at Wynter. "So you and Rafe—how's that going?"

Wynter fingered her scar. "He's … we're …"

The women chuckled.

"That good, huh?" Daisy said.

Helen caught Jack's eye, indicating that she wanted to talk with him.

"Excuse me, ladies, but I'm gonna snag my handsome"—she gave Sandy a wink—"son for a moment."

Wynter frowned as she watched her aunt meet Jack by the pond.

"Iris looks so happy. I'm glad we came," Gabby said with a smile as she watched the kids play tug-of-war with Rufus.

"Yes, she really got a kick at showing Jeff and Tommy how to draw. The spinach dip you brought was delicious." Wynter then glanced at the men at the grill. "They look so serious. You would think they were cooking prime rib over there," she said with a laugh.

※

Helen met Jack by the pond.

"What's up, Mom?"

"My sister called me the other night."

"How's Aunt Marguerite doing?"

"Good, good." Helen looked up at Jack. "She told me that Wynter is in danger. That this danger may be from her father."

Jack hugged his mother. "Look, I know you think Wynter's father had something to do with Brenna's death, but I'm telling you it was Neil, her second husband. I don't have any physical proof, but I know in my gut it was Neil. As far as I know, Wynter's father has never had any contact with Wynter. Why would he now?"

Helen glanced worriedly at Wynter before turning

her attention back to Jack. "I don't know, Jack. You know how these things go. You have pieces to the puzzle, but not the complete picture. I don't know how Martin is involved …" Helen hesitated. "I mean, Wynter's father. You're right. He has never sought contact with Wynter. But Marguerite is sure Wynter's father is involved. Maybe not directly, but …"

Helen shrugged. "Your father thinks we should wait and see what happens. That we shouldn't tell Wynter about her father. And I agree. She's been through so much. I just don't want her getting hurt by her father as well. I am only telling you because I want you to keep a close eye on Wynter and see if you can pick up any chatter about her father."

"You know I am not okay about keeping things from Wynter. She has the right to know about him, but I'll abide by your wishes. I'll keep an eye out for Wynter as well as her father."

Helen smiled at Jack and squeezed his hand. "Thanks, Jack."

※

"Everything okay, Aunt Helen?" Wynter asked when Helen rejoined the group.

Helen sat down next to Daisy. "Everything's fine, dear," Helen said with a serene smile. She turned to Daisy. "You must tell me how you streak your hair. It looks marvelous."

※

Wynter saw Sandy looking at Jack longingly. "He really likes you, you know," Wynter said.

Sandy jumped, and her face flushed red. "What?"

"Jack. He really likes you. He had the biggest crush on you in high school. He was really pissed at Kimberly when she told you those lies, but Jack was afraid you wouldn't believe him. He never dated or went out with Kimberly, you know," Wynter said as she fingered her scar.

Sandy gave Wynter an assessing look. "She always did pick on you when we were in school. I never understood it. You're right. She said some awful things, and I wouldn't have believed Jack then. I mean, I was no beauty queen, and Jack was the most popular boy in school, so why wouldn't he take what she was offering?"

"She certainly was possessive of Jack. She even said nasty things about Jack's and my relationship. I never understood her cruelty. It always seemed liked she wanted what she couldn't have." Wynter shrugged. "Anyway I just wanted to tell you that Jack always liked you and wanted to, you know, get to know you better," Wynter said and blushed. "Not that I'm matchmaking or anything."

Wynter blew out her breath in relief when Jack yelled, "Burgers and hot dogs are done. Come and get it."

※

Wynter watched as Rafe bagged up the last of the garbage. "Thanks for helping me clean up this mess. I love having people over, but the cleanup I can do without."

"No problem. You throw a mean party. Everyone

seemed like they had a good time. I didn't realize how close Jack and Hank are."

"Yeah, best buddies since high school. They also served together in the marines."

"Daisy and Hank are an odd couple, her with her crazy streaked hair and him so quiet. I would never have imagined them together."

"I think that is why it works so well. They complement each other." Wynter looked out over the pond and wrapped her arms about her. Her gaze was distant.

"Iris really had a good time. I think she got along great with Sandy's boys. Seeing her today, you would never have guessed what happened to her last year. It was good to see John and Gabby enjoying themselves as well." Rafe stood behind Wynter and gently pulled her into his embrace.

"Is there something between Sandy and your cousin?"

"I think they both want there to be something. In high school, Jack asked out Sandy, but Kimberly, the mayor's daughter, sabotaged it by telling Sandy that Jack was only going out with her because of some kind of bet. Kimberly wanted Jack for herself, but he never did like her, and he never gave her the time of day. Jack took it pretty hard when he realized how hurt Sandy was because of Kimberly's cruelty. He never forgave her for it. It may not seem like it, but Jack's kind of shy. I just hope he gets up his nerve and asks her out. I think they would be great together."

Wynter called out to Rufus, then glanced over she shoulder at Rafe. "Are you going to stay tonight?"

Rufus ran up to them and bumped his head against

their legs as he begged for attention. Rafe absently rubbed Rufus behind the ear, then turned Wynter around in his arms, and took her lips in a scorching kiss.

"There isn't any place I'd rather be," he said as Rufus danced around them.

※

The following evening, Rafe and Wynter were cozied up on the couch in John and Gabby's living room, with Iris lying on pillows on the floor watching TV.

"Thanks for keeping me company. This is a big step for Gabby," Rafe said as his cell phone started ringing. He picked up his phone and checked who was calling before answering. He smiled. "Hi, Gabby. How's dinner going? Good, good … yes, Iris is fine. She's right here. We're watching *Beauty and the Beast* … Okay," Rafe said as he motioned Iris over. "Iris, your mom wants to talk to you."

"Hi, Mommy. I'm fine, Mommy. Okay, I will." Iris handed the phone back to Rafe and went back to the pillows, falling on them with a thud.

"Feel better, kiddo? Good. Wynter and I have everything under control, so take your time and enjoy yourself. You're doing great, kiddo." Rafe disconnected the call, put his phone back on the coffee table, and put his arm around Wynter. "At least she's trying." He sighed.

Wynter snuggled against Rafe. "It will get easier as she continues taking these baby steps. Like you said, this is a big step for Gabby. Just don't be too surprised if they come home early," Wynter said with a smile. She glanced up at Rafe and bit her lower lip. "Do you want to … ummm … come over when Gabby and John get home?"

Rafe leaned down and kissed Wynter. "I'd love to."

❦

Oscar hung up the phone and frowned. This was really bad. *How the hell did DNA get left at the crime scene last month, and why am I only now hearing of this? Christ, what a mess.* His fucking crew really screwed things up. The feds had not only his brother's name but his name as well. *What a fucking mess.*

He rubbed the back of his neck. *If the man ever finds out that the feds are on to him.* He shuddered.

Oscar leaned back into his chair and wiped the sweat trickling down his neck with his hand. He had to think and make this right. He grabbed his phone and punched in a number.

"Yeah … Joey, get your ass over here now."

❦

Jack walked into the Blue Diner, found his cousin at their usual booth, and slid in across from her. She glowed with happiness. Her eyes sparkled, reflecting the deep purple of the sweater she wore.

"Hey, cuz, you look gorgeous," Jack said and smirked. "I hear Rafe's been staying at your house for the past two weeks. He the reason you look so happy?"

A goofy smile brightened her face. "I never really let myself believe …" Wynter shrugged and ran her finger down her scar. "He's okay with my scars. He's willing to accept my gift. The last two weeks, well, I've never felt this way before."

Jack sat back in the booth and saw the doubt in his cousin's eyes. "You don't really believe he loves you, do you?"

Wynter shook her head and then took a sip of her tea. "Love doesn't have anything to do with it. He's never experienced the visions. You know how disturbing they can be." Wynter looked up at Jack. "Not many people can handle my gift, ya know?"

Jack looked away from Wynter. His eyes widened, and a chuckle escaped. "Daisy, what happened to the purple stripes?"

Daisy smiled and walked to their table. "Hey, sugar, you want your usual?" Then she glanced at Wynter. "Anything else for you, honey?"

Wynter looked up at Daisy and smiled. "Blue looks good on you, Daisy. And yes, I would love another cup of tea."

Daisy's bleached blonde hair sported streaks of blue. She patted her hair. "You got it." She spotted Hank behind the counter and gave him her brightest smile, blowing him a kiss.

Jack and Wynter sat in silence while they waited for Daisy to return with their drinks.

"Here you go, sugar. If you need anything else, you just give me a holler," Daisy said with a wink. She left them to wait on other tables.

Jack took a sip of his coffee. "You think Rafe will freak when he sees you have a vision of something lost?"

Wynter smiled sadly. "I'd like to think he won't,

but he told me about a crazy ex of his who allowed superstition to rule her life." Wynter bit her lower lip. "But I think there is something else going on. Something else is bothering him." Wynter rested her chin in her palm. "I think something else has colored his view of … well, you know. So no. I don't think he will react well to my visions and now these crazy dreams. I worry about what would happen if I have one of those crazy dreams while he is with me."

Jack smiled. "You're in love with him, aren't you?"

Wynter closed her eyes and sighed. "Yes."

Wynter jumped when the bell above the door tinkled and a new customer entered the diner. Jack glanced up and saw Roger Thorpe heading their way.

"Hey, Roger. How you doin'?" Jack asked.

"Hey, Jack, I noticed that you and Wynter were here." Roger smiled at Wynter. "Hey, Wynter, I just wanted to let you know that I fixed your car, and she's ready whenever you're able to pick her up."

Wynter returned Roger's smile. "Thanks, Roger. I'll stop by later this afternoon. How's Rosie doing?"

"She's keeping busy at the bookstore. She's restarting story time. This Sunday is the big day. She sure is looking forward to it. It'll be the first one since, you know, when that Richards kid was kidnapped. She was really broken up when that kid was taken like that from her store. I told her it wasn't her fault," Roger said.

"Of course it wasn't her fault," Wynter said, shivering as she felt a sudden chill.

"That's right. I got the flyer in the mail. I am so glad

that she decided to have story time again. I know the kids have missed it," Jack said.

"Well, I just wanted to tell you that your car is ready. I got to get back to the garage. See you later," Roger said and went to pick up his takeout.

"Right, see you later, Roger." Wynter frowned as a sense of foreboding chilled the air.

※

"Dammit, Joey," Oscar said as he slammed his fist on the desk. "I am fucking tired of hearing your excuses."

"There's nothing 'cause nobody's talking," Joey said as he wiped the sweat off his face.

Oscar sat back in his chair. "The boss isn't returning my phone calls. We gotta fix things with him. I don't see we have much choice. We'll snatch another kid from that same area. The man will appreciate getting a replacement kid. The customer wasn't too happy that he was missing a kid. We'll have a chance to draw out that fucking rat bastard who squealed and killed my brother. Have that guy you used the last time to find another kid. We need this, Joey. No more fuckups. We need to get the ransom this time and then disappear for a while."

"You tellin' the man our plans?"

"Naw, it'd be better if we had something to give him. This is our mess to clean up. You let me worry about the man. You just do your job."

"Sure thing, boss. I'm on it."

※

Sandy eyed Rafe and wondered what kind of boss he would be in the long run. So far he seemed capable and was easy to get along with.

"Your day is light today. Joanne Sullivan is your first appointment. She wants to make changes to the custody agreement that Mr. Sullivan's attorney drafted. The Reeds have an appointment to sign their new wills, and Mr. Hooper wants to discuss a zoning problem with you after lunch."

"Are there any issues I should know about?" Rafe asked.

Sandy pursed her lips and contemplated if she should tell him about Joanne Sullivan's volatile nature, but then if he read the file, he would know there was a good reason why Mr. Sullivan was granted full custody.

Shaking her head, she said, "No, I can't think of any problems you need to know about." She had decided not to say anything about Joanne.

"Good. It looks like the whole week is pretty light." Rafe smiled.

Sandy cleared her throat. "Oh, I almost forgot. Mayor Randal called earlier this morning and wants to have lunch with you sometime this week. I think he's looking to see if you might be interested in representing the town."

Rafe rubbed his jaw. "Is this something I should talk to Walter about?"

Sandy shook her head. "Walter never wanted to get that involved with the town's politics. I don't think he would be adverse to you taking on the township as a client, but you would really need to ask him. Also, it would depend on how political you are. Do you want to get involved in small-town politics?"

"Hmm. Good question. It's certainly something to think about. Schedule a lunch for later this week. It'll give me time to think about whether or not being involved in small-town politics is something I want to do, and I think I'll call Walt for his opinion before I make any decisions." Rafe said with a smile.

❦

Charles Randal, the mayor of Black Falls, came from money and was tastefully dressed in a gray Armani suit. He was a slender man in his early fifties. A diamond ring graced his pinky finger. He lightly stroked his mustache as his secretary walked into his office.

"Lunch has been scheduled this Thursday with Rafe Wolf."

Charles raised his eyebrow. "Excellent, Silvie. What do you know about Mr. Wolf?"

Silvie always knew the latest gossip. It was her job to know what was going on in town. "Well, let's see. Mr. Wolf moved here to be closer to his sister, Gabby Richards. I heard there was some bad business with his partner from his old firm. Oh! And he's been seen around town with Wynter Malone."

Charles already knew of Rafe's interest in Wynter. It was one of the reasons he wanted to meet the man. There was no need for Silvie to know that though.

"Good work, Silvie. Please make reservations at Second Chances for our lunch on Thursday."

Silvie looked up from her notebook. "Consider it done. Do you need anything else?"

Charles shook his head. "No, that's all for now."

"Very good, sir." Silvie walked out of the office and closed the door gently behind her.

Charles leaned back into his chair and contemplated the call he had received from the big man. Owing the boss man was not a position he wanted to be in. *Damn that hooker who set me up. If that tape gets out, there go my political dreams.* Now he had to spy on that fuckup Oscar and report to the big man, one scary dude. *How stupid can one man be?*

He still couldn't believe that Oscar pulled a job here in Black Falls and then did that kidnapping one month ago a few towns over. Tourist season was over. Collecting ransom was never a good idea. Money could always be traced. The fool actually thought he could get away with stealing from the boss man. Now he had to report on him without drawing attention to himself. *What a goddamn mess.*

What interested him, what he might be able to use to his advantage, was the boss's request to keep an eye on Wynter Malone. There was more to this Malone thing. He just needed to find out what that was. It could just be the ticket he needed to get out from under the boss's thumb.

That's what I get for trusting family. It's just my dumb luck that my cousin is a crime lord.

❃

Rafe woke up in a cold sweat. *Damn, not this again.* Thankfully Wynter still slumbered by his side. Rafe gingerly got out of bed, not wanting to wake Wynter. He quietly walked down the stairs to the kitchen and guzzled a few glasses of water. Still feeling restless, Rafe went out to the back porch and sat on the swing. Hearing Rufus whine, Rafe got up and let him out.

"Hey, boy, you gonna keep me company?" he said as he rubbed Rufus's head.

Is it any wonder that I would dream of my grandfather? His grandfather, shaman of the Nanticoke Lenni-Lanape tribe, told him he had a gift for tapping into the dreams of others. Some called it dream walking. He called it creepy. Entering the dreams of another could be dangerous, especially when one had the power to change a dream.

He could deny it all he wanted, but a year ago, he knew he walked Wynter's dreams. Although this was the first time that a bond had been created between him and the person whose dreams he walked. He did his best to suppress his ability as he knew how fatally dangerous the outcome of dream walking could be. As much as he wanted Wynter in his life, no matter what he wanted, he could not allow his ability to resurface.

God, I've fallen in love with her. I just can't go through that again, Rafe thought as he watched the sun rise with Rufus lying on his feet.

❧

Wynter looked down from the balcony at the man she loved, wanting to offer him comfort, but she knew that he would have to deal with whatever troubled him on his own. *If only he would trust me enough and tell me what's bothering him.* She felt the barrier he placed between them, knowing how easily she could lose him in this silent battle that he fought on his own.

12

Jack looked out the window of his office and watched as Sandy pulled up in front of the Jeffrey & Wolf Law Firm. Sandy was in the process of removing a case of copy paper from the trunk of her car when Jack came up behind her.

"Here, let me get that for you." Jack grabbed the box out of the trunk.

Sandy jumped. "Geesh, you scared the bejesus out of me," Sandy said as a blush spread across her face.

This always happened whenever she encountered Jack Johnson. *God, the crush I had on him in high school.* Her face burned even redder when she thought of the fiasco of him asking her out. How she could have believed Kimberly Randal, Charles Randal's daughter, when she knew Kimberly wanted Jack for herself, she'd never know.

It wasn't until years later that Sara, Jack's sister, told her there was no bet. Jack would never have made a bet like that. Jack really had wanted to date her. She was so mean to Jack that day. Her actions that day still embarrassed her. She had said some pretty nasty things to him, like "entitled asshole" or "God's gift to women." Whatever she said, it was really bad. When she realized that she had hurt Jack, it was too late.

Sandy slowly turned around to face him. "Jack, I …" Sandy looked down at her hands. "I mean, what are …" She sighed and gave Jack a shy smile. "Thank you, Jack."

Jack returned Sandy's smile. "Just tell me where you want it."

Sandy rummaged through her purse and pulled out her keys to unlock the office door. "Just put it by the copier," she said and then went in and turned on the lights.

Jack put the box down by the copier. He coughed and rubbed the back of his neck. "I was wondering if maybe you'd like to go out for dinner this weekend."

Stunned, Sandy's mouth dropped open as she stared at Jack.

"I mean, don't feel like you have to …"

"No, no. I mean, yes, I would love to go out to dinner," Sandy stammered and played with the sleeve of her sweater.

A big grin broke across Jack's face. "Great, how about Saturday, say around six?"

Sandy blew out a breath. "Yeah, six is perfect."

"Great, I'll see you then," Jack said. "Well, until Saturday then."

He left the office whistling. Sandy leaned against the copier, feeling a little shocked by what just happened. "Oh my God! I got a date with Jack," she said out loud.

She walked to the front window and watched him cross the street and enter his office. She smiled and pinched herself. *I have a date with Jack.*

※

Wynter, dressed in faded blue jeans and a green flannel shirt, was in her studio working on illustrations for a children's book. She wasn't too happy with the dragon she was drawing. She decided to put the drawing aside when the doorbell rang. Rufus scrambled to find purchase on the hardwood floor as he rushed downstairs.

Wynter followed Rufus and opened the door. "Oh my God! Sara, it's so good to see you. Come in. Come in. Rufus, stop that. Let her walk in the door. What are you doing home? Are you here on vacation?"

Wynter looked up at Sara and was startled again by her haunting beauty. Sara was taller and a little curvier than Wynter was. She had the same mass of black curly hair and Jack's sky-blue eyes that were shadowed, eyes that hide an old sadness.

Sara laughed. "Take a breath, Wynter. It's good to see you too. And hello, Rufus. I'm glad to see you as well," she said, trying to avoid being slobbered on by Rufus. It was a good thing she was wearing jeans and a navy-blue sweater instead of her usual uniform of black slacks, white button-down shirt, and black jacket.

Wynter felt a sudden chill run down her spine. She rubbed her arms. "Have you seen your mom and dad? What about Jack? Does he know you're back in town?" Wynter asked as they walked into the kitchen.

"I just came from Mom and Dad's. I'll see Jack later at dinner tonight. Now come on and give your old cousin a hug."

Wynter gave Sara a hard hug, not wanting to let go.

Sara pulled back. "I hear you have a new man in your life, and I'm hoping you'll bring him to dinner tonight."

"I wouldn't miss it. You'll love Rafe. He's just wonderful." Wynter sighed. "Come on into the kitchen, and I'll get us both an iced tea."

"That would be great. So this Rafe is wonderful, but …" Sara said as her gaze became unfocused, like she was seeing something else.

"Why don't we go out onto the back porch?" Wynter asked as she pulled on a gray wool sweater. "Soon it'll be too cold to sit outside."

Sara took a long look at Wynter. "You've fallen in love. So what's the problem?"

Wynter watched as a leaf fell to the ground. "He's struggling with something, and I fear it's going to pull us apart. Did Jack tell you about these crazy dreams I'm having now? I mean, it's bad enough when I go blank because I am seeing where something is, but now I have these horrible nightmares, vague premonitions or something."

Sara pulled Wynter into a hug. "You've met your dream man. Sometimes that can have an effect upon your gift. Things will work out. You'll see." She took a deep breath. "It's so beautiful here," Sara said as they settled back into the swing to watch Rufus chase squirrels while they sipped their iced tea.

The Johnsons' dining room was bathed in a warm golden glow and rang with the laughter of its occupants.

"The whole family is together. You couldn't have given me a better gift," Helen said and smiled as she looked around the table.

"It's good to be home," Sara said, and she smiled at her mother.

"How long are you staying?" Jack asked.

"It depends on how the business end of my visit goes."

"And you're not going to share what the business might be?" Wynter asked, laughing.

Sara smiled. "No, I'm not, Little Miss Nosy." Sara turned and smiled at Rafe. "So how are you settling in? It must be a big change from the city."

Rafe took a sip of his Irish coffee. "Actually it's going better than I imagined. I love the diversity of my caseload, and Sandy has been a tremendous help. I definitely made the right move."

"I hear you are having lunch with Mayor Randal tomorrow?" Jack winked at Wynter.

Sara frowned. "A man to be wary of."

"Am I missing something?" Rafe asked.

"Naw. Randal is what some might say a consummate politician. That's all." Stuart looked at Helen quizzically. "Doesn't he have family that has criminal connections?"

Helen turned to her husband. "Stuart!"

"Mayor Randal had a problem with Aunt Helen's herbal remedies and tried to shut her side business down. But there was nothing he could really do. Aunt Helen has her NCCAOM and does not claim to diagnose or cure diseases. It was a waste of time and a waste of the taxpayers' money, and he knew that. He left a bad taste behind with his actions," Wynter explained. She wrinkled her nose. "Definitely not a nice man."

"Yeah, he knew there was really nothing that he could do, but still he went ahead, costing us a lot of money. As you know, attorneys ain't cheap," Stuart said. "So yeah, he made no friends here." A spark of mischief lit Stuart's eyes. "He never really got over losing you, darling."

Helen laughed. "Oh, poppycock! We had one date, and it was a horror. We both knew it, and that was that."

Sara, Jack, and Wynter looked at one another and burst out laughing.

Sara wiped the tears from her eyes. "They are always teasing each other. Even though everyone knows it was love at first sight, right, Pop?"

Stuart smiled lovingly at his wife. "You got that right."

※

Wynter and Sara were on the back porch as Rufus marked his territory around the backyard.

"What do you think?" Wynter asked.

Sara glanced at Wynter. "He's in love with you, but you're right. There is something that's stopping him from fully committing to you."

"I just hope we survive what's coming." Wynter looked at Sara. "That's why you are here, isn't it?"

"Unfortunately, yes," Sara said sadly.

She turned to look at the full moon. *Some things cannot be changed*, she thought.

※

Rafe and Wynter walked into the diner as Kimberly Randal and her husband were leaving. "Oh, look, honey. If it isn't our own little town freak?" Kimberly said to her husband. "How's tricks, Wynter?"

Wynter bared her teeth at Kimberly in a facsimile of a smile. "Always a pleasure to see you, Kimberly," Wynter said as she pushed past Kimberly and walked to the booth where Jack waited for her and Rafe.

Rafe gave Kimberly a cool look and followed Wynter. He slid in next to her and then glanced back to watch Kimberly leave with a look of disdain on his face. "Does that happen a lot? People calling you a freak?"

Wynter took a sip of Jack's water before answering. "No, but Kimberly was my biggest tormentor in school, and she's never outgrown her bitchy side, if you know what I mean," she said with a shrug.

"She thinks because she's the mayor's daughter she can do no wrong, and she is awful to most people," Jack said.

"Let's not worry about Kimberly. The best way to get to her is not to let what she says upset me," Wynter said with a nod.

❦

Rafe and Wynter were sitting on the balcony off Wynter's bedroom, snuggled under a blanket, enjoying the starlit night and warmed brandy. Rafe took Wynter's hand in his and rubbed the back of her knuckles.

"Did that happen a lot to you when you were younger?"

Wynter looked over at Rafe. "What?"

"You know, people calling you a freak and treating you like an outcast?"

Wynter took a sip of her brandy and then glanced up at Rafe. "School was rough, but Sara did her best to include me in her group of friends. It wasn't as bad as it could have been. Most people were nice once they got used to me, but some like Kimberly just always had something nasty to say. I think it had something to do with her boyfriend at the time. I tutored him for a semester, and we became friends. She couldn't stand for Brody to pay attention to anyone but her. Let's not talk about high school antics. It's a beautiful night, and I can think of other things I would rather be doing," Wynter said with a wicked smile gracing her lips. She took Rafe's brandy and put it on the table along with hers.

Subtly, the atmosphere changed. Rafe's gaze heated as Wynter's smile ignited his passions. Wynter's pulse increased as she turned to Rafe, who pulled her closer, and his lips captured hers. His tongue thrust into her mouth in a searing kiss. Desire slammed into her. Emotions exploded within her, exciting and frightening her all at once. Yes, she had her dreams, and they shared an undeniable chemistry, but she was still wary of his intentions and if he would ever be able to accept her. *If he would ever love me.*

"No, no, sweetheart. Don't pull away," Rafe said as he breathed kisses down her neck. "This is right. There is nothing to be afraid of. Trust me. I have never felt anything that felt so good and so right."

Rafe stood up and swept Wynter into his arms, carrying her into the bedroom and depositing her on the bed. Rafe's mouth followed as he unbuttoned Wynter's shirt, pushing it off her shoulders. He swirled his tongue around her nipple before taking it into his mouth, gently sucking it like a ripe raspberry.

"God, you taste so good. I can't get enough of you," he murmured.

Pleasure swept through Wynter as she arched up for more of Rafe's touch. Wynter's fingers flew to the buttons on his shirt. Quickly she unbuttoned his shirt and pushed it off his shoulders. Rafe took her hand and placed it upon his nipple.

"That's it, sweetheart. Pinch it. Yeah, just like that." His voice was raspy with desire.

Wynter's breath caught at the raw beauty of Rafe's pleasure. She stroked her hand down his body and took his throbbing erection in her hand.

"God, Wynter, you're killing me," Rafe moaned.

Rafe's fingers found Wynter's wet heat, and her thighs spread wider, giving Rafe greater access. "You're so wet for me. It's like your body was made for me."

Wynter was drowning in the heat of Rafe's gaze. "Rafe, I need you. Please do it now, Rafe. I need you inside me."

Rafe nibbled his way down her body and replaced his fingers with his tongue. He suckled on her sweetness, licking and sucking, feasting on her lush nectar. Wynter grasped his hair within her hands, holding him to her as she felt pleasure unlike anything she had ever known.

"Yes, Rafe, more, I need more …" Wynter screamed as her body exploded and wave after wave of pleasure rolled through her body.

Slowly Rafe aligned himself at her drenched entrance and thrust into her velvet heat. "God, baby, you're so tight. I don't think …"

Wynter's vagina tightened around him, milking him. Throwing his head back in pleasure, Rafe gasped as he thrust harder and deeper into her.

He moaned as he came. "Mine, forever," he cried.

Wynter sighed. *Yes, mine*, she thought. Exhausted, replete, and feeling as if her empty spaces were now filled, Wynter snuggled into Rafe's embrace and fell asleep.

Adjusting himself so he wouldn't crush her, Rafe fell asleep with a smile and feeling like he was finally home.

※

Wynter fisted her hands as she looked through the window. Two men stood over a child who wore a hood. She couldn't identify the child.

"Where are we?"

Startled, Wynter turned and saw Rafe standing next to her. "Rafe, what are you doing here?"

Rafe looked around. Everywhere he looked was dark, except for the window. "I don't know where here is."

Wynter touched Rafe's arm. "You're in my dream. Those two men are going to kidnap that child. That's where you are. What I want to know is how you got here. How are you in my dream?"

Rafe tried to focus on the scene through the window. "Why is everything so blurry?"

Wynter looked back at the scene through the window.

"Sometimes the picture is not in focus. But Rafe, how are you here in my dream?"

Rafe looked at Wynter and saw her shiver. "You're freezing. Why is it so cold here?" Rafe gathered Wynter in his arms, trying to warm her.

Wynter put her hand on Rafe's chest. "I don't know why it's so cold here. These dreams are kind of new for me, but so far they're usually cold." Wynter looked up at Rafe. "How are you here, Rafe?" she asked again.

Rafe hugged Wynter close to him, gently rubbing her arms.

Color suddenly flooded Wynter's senses, making her dizzy. She clutched at Rafe's shoulders to steady herself as the dream faded.

"Oh my God! What just happened?" Wynter whispered.

Breathing heavy, she looked up at Rafe. "I have to call Jackson. I need to tell him …"

"Tell him what? We couldn't see the faces of the kidnappers clearly. The child had a hood over his head. What exactly can we tell Jack?"

"But I need my pencils and … and I need my drawing pad. Sometimes things are clearer if I draw them."

"All right, sweetheart. You keep them in this drawer, right?" Rafe leaned over and opened the end table drawer, pulling out a drawing pad and pencil. "Here you go, baby. You draw what you saw, and I'll go make something hot for you to drink. You feel like ice."

Rafe walked slowly down the stairs. *God, I've walked Wynter's dream. Deeps breaths. You can handle this*, he thought. *No, I am not a danger to Wynter. What could I possibly say to her? Now she knows I can enter her dreams.* He didn't know if he were ready to talk about his dream walking or his father. *What a mess*, he thought.

Rafe walked into the kitchen. He filled the teapot with water and set it to boil on the stove. With his mind racing, he blankly stared at the teapot. He needed to pull himself together. He didn't like how cold Wynter got from her dream vision.

The teapot boiled, and he fixed Wynter a cup of chamomile tea instead of the Earl Grey. She needed something to calm her down, not rev her up. *I'm not really looking forward to our conversation about my dream walking*, he thought. His body tensed. *God, what could I say to her?*

※

Rafe returned to the bedroom with a mug of chamomile tea and put it on the nightstand next to the bed. Wynter sat in the middle of the bed with papers strewn all around her. He picked up a few of the drawings and compared them.

"Wynter, stop. You've drawn the same picture at least fifty times. I have something hot for you to drink. Please—"

"Rafe," Wynter said weakly as she banged her head back against the bed board. "It's not enough. I get these stupid glimpses, and they're not enough. That child will be kidnapped. Why can't I ever get a clearer picture of

GIFT OF DREAMS

what is going to happen? This is so frustrating." A tear ran down her face. Her hands fisted in the bed covers.

Rafe put down the drawings he held and leaned over Wynter. "Baby, please don't cry. Gifts often come with a downside. Some things about the future are immutable. I know you will find this kid when the time comes, just like you found Iris." Rafe wiped the tears off her face.

Winter sniffled, grabbed a tissue from the box of tissues on the nightstand next to the bed, and wiped her nose. She patted the spot next to her on the bed. "Come sit next to me and tell me how you got into my dream, or is it a vision?"

Rafe sat next to Wynter, took her in his arms, and leaned against the headboard. His stomach knotted with tension.

Closing his eyes, he sighed. "Dream walking. I haven't walked another's dreams in years. I should have known I would be pulled into your vision dreams. I mean we do share dreams."

"You've had dreams about us too?" Wynter said as her face blazed red. "You … you never said anything," Wynter stammered.

"You never said anything to me about your dreams either," Rafe replied.

"But those dreams were so, so intimate."

Rafe smiled. His amber eyes burned hot with remembered desire. "You mean erotic, don't you?"

Wynter's eyes widened in shock. "You mean that you … that we … how could you share my dreams?" Wynter whispered.

Rafe traced Wynter's lower lip with his thumb. "I

don't understand our bond, but it's strong. You invited me into your dreams. Our gifts are similar. Maybe that has something to do with it."

Wynter had a flash of insight. "You deny your gift. Why?" Wynter felt a little lost and confused. "How come you never said anything to me? I feel the wall you've put between us … I feel … God, I feel like such an idiot. You don't trust me at all, do you? I told you about my visions. I shared my scars with you, and all you've done is build a wall between us. Did you think I wouldn't understand?" Wynter struggled out of Rafe's arms and went into the bathroom. She grabbed another tissue and blew her nose.

Rafe stumbled out of bed and followed Wynter into the bathroom. "It's not that I don't trust you. I do. My gift … my gift is dangerous." Rafe fisted his hand. "You're damn right I didn't tell you. What if I walked into your dreams and I ended up hurting you or worse? How could I live with that?" Rafe stormed out of the bathroom, gathering his clothes.

Wynter followed him out of the bathroom. "What are you doing?"

"What does it look like I'm doing? I'm getting dressed. I thought …" Rafe sank onto the edge of the bed. "I thought it was contained. We shared erotic dreams, yeah, but that was it. I won't walk your dreams, but tonight … dammit, tonight I walked your vision dream. I could have hurt you."

Wynter knelt before Rafe, taking his hands into hers. "What are you talking about? You gave me comfort. You took the chill away. You didn't come close to hurting me."

Rafe caressed Wynter's cheek. "One wrong step. One

small change is all it takes. I can't take that chance with you." Rafe continued to put on his clothes.

"Rafe, talk to me. Tell me what has you so terrified of your gift."

Rafe leaned down and kissed Wynter gently on the lips. "I can't go through that again, Wynter. I will not hurt another person I love." Rafe stood after putting on his boots. "Look, I gotta go. I can't be responsible for your death too. It's just too much." Rafe felt as if the walls were closing in on him.

No, not again, he thought. He looked wildly around the room.

"Rafe, talk to me."

Rafe ran his hand through his hair, feeling the pressure build within him. "What do you want me to say, Wynter? I killed my father in a dream, okay? Are you happy now? I will not take that chance with you. I … I can't see you anymore. It would kill me if anything happened to you because of my gift. I gotta go," Rafe said again and walked out, slamming the door behind him.

※

Wynter's eyes burned as she watched Rafe leave. She sat back on her bed, drew in her legs, and wrapped her arms around them. Rufus laid down on her feet.

"What just happened? How could he think he killed his father?" Wynter asked as she looked down at Rufus. "I guess it's just you and me, Rufus. What would I do without you? You don't care about whether or not I have visions. You don't make dumb excuses, like oh, I killed my father with my gift. Does he think I'm stupid? I can't believe he's blaming his gift for not wanting to be with me. You just love me as I am, don't you, boy? And you don't lie to me."

Rufus curled up next to her and licked her hand. Wynter laid her head on her knees. Tears fell silently down her cheeks.

※

The waiter placed a glass of wine before Sandy. "Thank you," she said with a smile.

Jack smiled as the waiter put down a whisky neat in front of him. He gazed at Sandy. She looked beautiful in her sleek black dress. Her hair was swept up in a french twist with her bangs feathered around her face, showing off her pearl earrings.

Jack cleared his throat. "Wynter said the new chef here is wonderful."

"Second Chances always has great food. I'm not surprised that John's new chef is wonderful. When Iris was kidnapped, I had doubts that the restaurant would survive."

"I agree. Gabby kind of fell apart, even though Iris was found. She seems to be doing much better now. Wynter told me she bakes at home and then runs the baked goods over here," Jack said.

Sandy nodded and smiled at Jack. "Yes, I think Rafe moving here has been wonderful for her."

Jack took a sip of his drink. "I'm so glad you agreed to have dinner. After that misunderstanding back in high school … well, I didn't think you'd ever want to have anything to do with me." Jack reached across the table and took Sandy's hand in his. "I had the biggest crush on you," Jack said, smiling.

Sandy blushed. "I … I had a crush on you too. I can't believe that I fell for Kimberly's lies." Sandy cleared her throat and took a sip of her wine. Her hand shook, and she quickly put down her drink. "I'm so sorry about the nasty things I said to you." Sandy gave Jack a nervous smile. "I was just so hurt."

"Hey, that was years ago, and now we have a second chance at getting to know each other. No apologies are necessary. I propose a toast to the future and getting to know each other better," Jack said as he raised his glass. "To second chances."

"Yes, here's to getting to know each other," Sandy said with a smile. "And second chances."

13

Gabby opened her front door, and her eyes widened. "Grandfather! What are you doing here? You never leave the reservation."

Joseph Wolf was dressed casually in jeans and a blue sweater. He wore his long graying brown hair in a braid. A duffel bag lay at his feet. "My grandchildren refuse to visit, so I must come to them. Will you invite me in?"

"Oh! Granddad, yes of course. Come in. Come meet your great-granddaughter." Gabby shook her head. "Do you want coffee? I just brewed a pot."

Joseph picked up his bag and followed Gabby. "That would be lovely, Gabriella."

They walked to the kitchen, and Gabby got another mug from the cabinet and poured coffee. "Black, right?"

"Good memory, Gabriella." Joseph put down his bag and smiled at Gabby.

Gabby handed her grandfather the mug and then went and topped off her own cup. "Sit, Granddad. I need to check on Iris. She should have been down by now." Gabby turned to run upstairs when Iris ran into her. "Iris." Gabby hugged her daughter. "Honey, come meet your great-grandfather. Granddad, this is my daughter, Iris. Iris, this is your great-grandfather, Joseph Wolf."

Joseph's amber eyes welled with tears. "She looks just like you. Well, except for her beautiful green eyes. Can you give your great-granddad a hug?"

Iris looked up at her mother. Gabby nodded to Iris. "Go on, honey. Give your great-granddad a hug. She has her daddy's eyes."

"Ah, yes, the cook. I remember now that he has green eyes." Iris pulled away from Joseph and went to stand by her mother. "Honey, why don't you go get your hairbrush and some scrunches so I can braid your hair?"

"We're still going to Wynter's after school, right?" Iris asked.

"Yes, we're going to Wynter's after school. Now go on and bring me your hairbrush so I can do your hair. It's almost time to leave for school."

Iris waved at Joseph and ran upstairs.

"She's beautiful, Gabriella."

"It's Gabby, Granddad. Everyone calls me Gabby."

Joseph looked at Gabby in disbelief. "Gabby," he said, wrinkling his nose in disdain. "I think not. I don't know what your mother was thinking when she gave you and Rafael those Spanish names."

Gabby rolled her eyes. "Not again, Granddad. Mom was Spanish."

"You and Rafael are of the people. You are Lenni-Lenape. You should have names that reflect your heritage."

Gabby sighed. "Granddad, your unrelenting stubbornness led to Mom and Dad leaving the reservation. Mom was not of the people. She had a right to her traditions. You pushed them away, and then you pushed away Rafe when we came to live with you after Mom died. My God, you don't even call John by his name. It's always 'the cook.' He's my husband, Granddad, and I love him. Why can't you accept that? Iris is our—"

"She is of the people. She has the gift, Gabriella, and she's one of the reasons I have come. Your brother is another reason I have come. He is killing his soul, Gabriella, and it must stop. You have no idea."

Gabby shook her head hard. "Granddad, Iris is my daughter. She is John's daughter, and she does not have the gift. I will not allow you to ruin her the way you did Rafe." Gabby frowned. "And by the way, what kind of name is Joseph? Certainly it's not a name of the people. So don't criticize Mom because she chose names that you didn't like."

Iris ran into the kitchen and handed Gabby the hairbrush and scrunchies. "Is everything okay, Mommy?" she asked as she gave Joseph a nervous look.

Gabby looked down at her daughter. "Yes, sweetie. Mommy and Granddad were just talking." She looked up at Joseph. "This conversation isn't over, Granddad. But right now I've got to get Iris ready for school."

"Let me braid my great-granddaughter's hair while you get dressed," Joseph said. His amber eyes warmed as he gazed at Iris.

Gabby looked at her grandfather and handed him the hairbrush and scrunchies. "Fine. It'll only take me a moment to get dressed." Gabby turned and went upstairs so she could get dressed to take Iris to school.

※

Joseph watched his granddaughter leave. The haunted look in her eyes saddened him. Joseph brushed Iris's hair and started the process of braiding her hair. "You know, I used to braid your mother's hair when she was your age." Joseph glanced down at Iris and smiled. Memories of the past softened his gaze.

Iris glanced back at her grandfather and gave him a tentative smile.

※

Sandy was typing a complaint for a personal injury case when the phone rang. "Good afternoon. Jeffrey and Wolf. Sandy speaking. May I help you? Sam … I don't understand. No, you can't see the boys. I don't have time for this, Sam. Why? How can you ask me that? You hit me! Then you went after Tommy. Look, Sam, I did not steal the kids. You refused to pay child support. You spent all of our savings on drugs. You slept with that bitch, Gloria. What do you want, Sam? That's never going to happen. The judge gave me full custody, and you do not have visitation rights. You refused to go to rehab, and without that, you still present a danger to the children. It took me two years to pull out of the financial hole that you put me in. Jeff and Tommy are just now really settling in and making friends. I will not allow you to mess with that. I'm sorry your mother is sick, but neither of you have made any effort to be part of their lives in the last two years, and I won't let you upset our lives now. Please don't call me again, not unless you have proof that you have completed rehab and are clean and sober."

Sandy disconnected the call and leaned back in her chair. *God, not again. I can't go through Sam's drama again*, she thought as she wiped the tears from her face. She had hoped she'd never hear from him again. He scared her, and there was no way she was letting that monster back into her son's lives. Any little thing could set off his violent temper, even when he was sober.

Rafe stepped out of his office. "Hey, Sandy, do you have that brief on the Miller case?" Rafe looked at Sandy and noticed her red eyes. "What's wrong, Sandy? Are you all right?"

Sandy got a Kleenex and blew her nose. "Yes. Sorry, Rafe." Sandy looked at the papers on her desk and found the Miller file. "Here you go, Rafe. The brief should be inside the file."

Rafe took the file from Sandy. "Thanks. Look, Sandy, I can see that you are upset. Please know that you can talk to me."

Sandy sniffled. "I've just had an upsetting phone call from my ex-husband. I haven't heard from him in two years. And well ... I just hope he doesn't call me again."

"Bad breakup?" Rafe asked.

"You could say that." She reached for another tissue and hiccupped. "Sorry," she mumbled as she wiped her nose. "Sam is my ex. Well, he's very violent and a drug addict. The court awarded me sole custody of my boys, and Sam isn't allowed to see them unless or until he has completed rehab and is sober. He's refused to go to rehab, and as far as I know, he is still using. Now he is asking to see the boys. His mom is sick, but I just can't subject my boys to his craziness. They are doing so well now."

Rafe frowned. "Is there anything I can do?"

Sandy shook her head and dabbed a clean tissue at her eyes. "No, I have legal custody of my boys and a restraining order against him. Other than that, there's really not much more I can do."

"Well, I'm here if you need anything. Maybe you should tell Jack. Let him know that Sam may be bringing trouble with him."

Sandy blushed. "No. I mean"—she hesitated and then took a deep breath—"okay, I'll talk with Jack. Please don't say anything to him. No one knows how bad things got between Sam and me, and I'd like to tell him myself."

Rafe gave Sandy a thoughtful look. "Sandy, you have nothing to be ashamed about. If you ex was violent, then that's on him."

"I know. It's just … I endangered my children by staying with him for so long. I … God I—"

"Sandy, you did nothing wrong. You left and divorced him. You protected your kids. Do you hear me? You did nothing wrong." Rafe put a comforting hand on her shoulder. "I want you to let me know if Sam calls you again. Okay? If he's not in compliance with the court order, then we can see what kind of legal action we can take against him, okay?"

Sandy sniffled. "Sure. I really appreciate it, Rafe."

Rafe smiled. "Now go take a break. I'll man the phones, okay?"

Sandy smiled and nodded. "Thanks, Rafe."

※

An hour later, Sandy knocked on Rafe's office door. "Come in."

"Hey, Rafe, your sister is here, and she looks pretty upset. Do you want me to send her in?"

Rafe frowned. "Yeah, send her in." Rafe looked at Sandy. "Also, hold my calls."

Sandy nodded. "Sure thing, Rafe."

Gabby walked into Rafe's office and waited for Sandy to close the door. She stood in front of Rafe's desk with her hands clenched into fists. "What happened last night?"

"What?" Rafe sat back in his chair.

"You came home around three this morning. You left for work before anyone else was awake. What happened last night?" Gabby asked. A scowl was on her face.

Rafe clenched and unclenched his fist. "Leave it alone, Gabby."

"No, Rafe. I will not leave it alone. Tell me what happened last night."

Rafe shuddered. "I dream-walked in Wynter's vision last night. There, you happy now? It's a miracle that I didn't kill her."

Gabby sank into the chair in front of Rafe's desk. "So that's why he's here."

"What? Who's here?"

Gabby looked up at Rafe. "Grandfather. He's here.

He said he came because of you." Gabby tore the tissue she held in her hands. "And because of Iris. He said she has the gift."

Rafe raked a hand through his hair. "What! There's no way that old man would leave the reservation."

Gabby snorted. "Wrong, Rafe. He's here. He's waiting for us at the house. He said you are killing your soul. What the hell does he mean by that, Rafe? Huh! Why did you come home at three in the morning, Rafe?"

"I broke things off with Wynter last night." Rafe stood up. "Don't you understand? I killed Dad in his dream. I walked into Wynter's vision. I could end up killing her too."

Gabby stared at Rafe. She jerked back her head. "Rafe, what the hell are you talking about? Dad died when you were fifteen. He died in that divvy hotel room after he gambled away all his money. You had nothing to do with Dad's death."

Rafe shook his head and started pacing. "Gabby, you know I have the ability to dream walk. I've never told you that the night Dad died I was there in his dream. I'm not sure how it really happened, but his dream changed, and he … he shot himself in the dream. Right in the goddamn head. He fucking killed himself in that dream. You know as well as I do. You die in your dream; you die in reality. They said it was a heart attack, but it wasn't. It was suicide."

Rafe stopped pacing and looked at Gabby. "I shouldn't have been in his dream, Gabby, but I was. I felt his dream change, and then he shot himself. I killed him, Gabby. It was my presence in his dream. My anger killed him."

Gabby leaned forward. "Rafe, Dad was a drunk who had a gambling problem. He had just lost everything he owned. He was a coward. After Mom died, he just left us with Granddad." Gabby took a deep breath. "He chose to drown his sorrows in alcohol. He chose to leave us. He took the easy way out, as always. You didn't kill Dad. He killed himself."

Rafe clenched his hands into fists. "No, no. Gabby, you weren't there. I felt his dream change. I stood frozen in place. I couldn't move. I couldn't stop him. He looked right at me when he shot himself. Why would he do that, Gabby? I still have nightmares about it. I see his eyes looking at me, accusing me."

Gabby shook her head. "That doesn't mean you changed the dream. You were fifteen for Christ's sake. I don't believe for one moment that you killed Dad. He was a fucking coward, Rafe, plain and simple. He chose the easy way out, like always. Is this what you and Granddad fought about? Is this why you moved in with Aunt Marie and Uncle Eduardo? Leaving me alone with Granddad for a whole goddamn year?" Gabby shouted.

"Gabby, I—"

"I don't want to hear it, Rafe. Yeah, a year later Granddad agreed to let me move in with Aunt Marie and Uncle Eduardo, but God, I hated living with him that year. I hated that you weren't there when I needed you."

Gabby wiped away the tears from her face. "Well, Granddad is here now, and I'm not dealing with him alone. I think ... yes ... I think he knows you broke up with Wynter. I don't know how this dream walking stuff works, and thank God I didn't get any of that shit. Granddad can help you."

Gabby stood up. "I can't believe you, Rafe. You found the woman of your dreams. You love her, and you just walked out on her." She held up her hand. "Don't even try to deny it. How can you just walk away from the woman you love? You walked away when I was thirteen, and it took a long time for me to forgive you. Don't make the same mistake with Wynter. Don't be a coward like Dad."

Gabby walked out of Rafe's office and quietly closed the door behind her.

※

Rafe sat back in his chair, stunned. Gabby thought he was a coward. Rafe got up, put on his jacket, and left his office. Rafe walked by Sandy's desk.

"Sandy, please cancel my appointments today. There's a family matter I need to take care of."

"You got it, Rafe," Sandy said as she cast a worried look in his direction.

※

Gabby stopped at Wynter's house. She sat in her car, worrying the tear in her pink sweater as she wondered what the hell she was doing here. *Oh yeah, I'm trying to save Rafe's relationship with Wynter. Well, no point in putting it off any longer*, she thought as she got out of the car.

Wynter opened the door before Gabby had a chance to knock. "I hope you don't mind, but I made some Earl Grey tea for us."

Gabby's eyes widened in surprise. "Yeah, sure."

"Come on in. Why don't we go out on the back porch? I left Rufus running around in the backyard."

Gabby cleared her throat. "Sounds good to me."

Rufus ran over to Gabby to be pet, bumping his massive head against her hand. Gabby laughed and bent down to give Rufus a hug. "I'm glad to see you too, Rufus."

Wynter smiled. "All right, Rufus. You've had your hug. Come sit by me," Wynter said as she patted the seat next to her on the porch swing. Rufus jumped up and plopped his big head in Wynter's lap. Wynter smiled at Gabby. "He's really just a big puppy."

Gabby laughed again. "I can see that."

Wynter reached for the teacup sitting on the table beside her and handed Gabby a cup. "So what's on your mind, Gabby? I thought you and Iris were coming over later?"

Gabby took a sip of tea and sighed. "How did you know I would be here this morning?"

Wynter ran her hands down Rufus's back. "Sometimes I just know things, little things really. Like maybe I need to make a full pot of tea because company's coming."

Gabby smiled. "It's wonderful you know. The tea. I never had Earl Grey before."

"It's the honey. So comforting, don't you think? So …" Wynter looked at Gabby and gave her a small smile.

Gabby cleared her throat. "I, ummm, saw Rafe this morning."

Wynter blushed and ran a finger down her scar. "Ah, so you know he walked out last night."

Gabby put her teacup down on the table. "That's what

I want to talk to you about. Rafe's got some crazy idea that he killed our father in a dream. I ... well, I don't have his gift, but I know my brother, and I know he didn't kill our father." Gabby bowed her head. "My grandfather showed up this morning, and I think he agrees with me. He said he came to help Rafe."

Gabby shrugged. "I guess I'm asking you to have some patience. To let Rafe work through this. I know ..." Gabby looked up at Wynter. "I know he loves you. Just don't give up on him. That's all I'm asking."

Wynter closed her eyes. A tear escaped and ran down her cheek.

※

Rafe stormed into Gabby's kitchen. "Grandfather, what are you doing here?"

"Rafael, it's good to see you," Joseph said as he drank in the sight of his grandson.

Rafe clenched his teeth. "Good to see me? Is that all you have to say? It's good to see me."

"No, but you are not yet ready to hear what I have to say."

Rafe took a deep breath, saw there was coffee, and poured himself a mug. He looked at his grandfather, whom he hadn't seen in years. He looked the same as he did the last time he saw him: long brown hair with silver running through it, pulled off his angular face in a braid. He was dressed in soft jeans and a brown sweater.

Rafe sighed. "Again, why are you here, Grandfather?"

Joseph got up from the kitchen table, walked over to

Rafe, and poured himself another cup of coffee. "Are you ready to talk about the night your father died?" Joseph calmly asked.

"There's nothing to talk about."

"You're wrong, Rafael. This conversation has been put off too long. I just hope … well, I hope it's not too late." Joseph looked down into his mug.

"Too late for what?"

Joseph shook his head. His eyes clouded over. "I did not believe that you would stay away for so long. We need to talk about the night you dream-walked your father's dream."

Rafe took a sip of his coffees and then shrugged. "What for?"

Joseph's head snapped up. "How about that, at the age of fifteen, you didn't have the control or the experience to change your father's dream or anyone else's for that matter? That a dream walker does not change another's dreams but helps guide those whose dreams they walk so they may change the dream?"

Rafe shook his head. "No, you told me that strong emotions could change a dream. When I entered Dad's dream, I was angry. I hated that he left us after Mom died. It was my anger, my hate, that changed Dad's dream and killed him."

Joseph sighed. "Yes, strong emotions can change a dreamscape, but only because the dream walker can influence the dreamer. You did not have the control to change a dreamscape through your emotions. Certainly you didn't have enough control to influence your father and make him shoot himself. Right after when you woke up, you told me that you felt paralyzed, that you couldn't move. Your father had complete control of the dream. He locked you into his dream and made you watch him kill himself. When you became paralyzed and couldn't move, rage and hate no longer fueled you, but fear and shock. Your father used your emotions against you that night and made you watch his death. I'll never understand why he did that to you, but he did."

"If that were the case, why didn't you tell me all this before?" Rafe demanded.

Joseph walked back to the kitchen table and wearily sank into the chair. He put down his mug and sighed. "You ran to your aunt and uncle's house before I could explain. Then you refused to talk to me. I kept waiting, thinking that, as you grew older, you would come to me for explanations. Instead you buried your emotions, fought, and suppressed your gift, and now you have put your soul in peril."

Joseph sighed again. "I must take the blame in this. Just as Gabriella has said, my stubbornness would not allow me to reach out to you. I knew you needed to understand about that night, but I wanted you to come to me. So here I am. I have come to right a mess made by your father."

Rafe took a sip of his coffee and then rubbed his neck. "To clean a mess, the saying is to clean a mess." Rafe corrected absently. He felt overwhelmed, angry, and a certain amount of relief. He didn't kill his father.

All those wasted years, carrying all that guilt—and for what? Rafe looked like he had been struck by lightning.

God, Wynter. What have I done? Rafe thought as he turned to leave. He had to find Wynter and explain.

Joseph eyed his grandson. "Ah, yes, to clean a mess. But now you need to concentrate on the woman you love. Danger surrounds her. You have to overcome your fear of dream walking. It will only be through your dream connection that you will be able to save her."

Rafe stopped and slowly turned around. "Grandfather, what the hell are you talking about?"

※

Jack walked into the Blue Diner and saw Sandy sitting at his favorite booth. He walked slowly toward her as he took in her quiet beauty. "Hey, sweetheart, how are you this afternoon?" he asked as he slid into the booth.

Sandy smiled as she played with the napkin on the table. "Hi, Jack."

"You look nervous. Is everything okay?"

She sighed. "I …" She took a deep breath. "I, yes, yes, something's wrong. Sam's been calling me and … well, I'm afraid he's going to try to see the boys. It's been over two years since he's seen them. They are finally adjusting to life without their dad and …" She shrugged and raised puffy eyes to Jack.

Jack's eyes narrowed. "I know he took all your money. Is there another reason why his seeing the boys upsets you?"

"It's …" Sandy took a sip of water and looked out the window. She sighed and turned to look at Jack. "It's not something I really talk about. But Sam has a violent temper. He hurt Tommy, and I don't trust him not to hurt both my boys. And it's not just his temper. Sam has a drug problem, and he refuses to go to rehab."

Jack frowned. "Do you have a current protection order against him?"

Sandy nodded. "Yes, I talked with Rafe to make sure everything is in place, but it's just paper. There is nothing to stop him from taking the boys and harming them. He seemed really desperate, and he scares me. I just felt ... I don't know. That I should tell you what is going on. I know there's not much you can do, but well ..." She shrugged again and looked down at her lap.

"Hey." Jack reached across the table and took her hand in his. "I understand. I'll keep an eye out. You call me if he continues to harass you, okay?"

Sandy smiled in relief. "Yes, I will definitely call you."

Jack squeezed Sandy's hand. Though he had questions, he could see how she was struggling to keep it together. "Well, now that's settled, why don't we order lunch?"

Sandy gave him a bright smile. "Yes, that sounds great."

※

Jack returned to his office, feeling troubled about Sandy's ex. Protection orders were good, but as she said, they were just paper and didn't always stop an abuser. He'd make some calls. He'd see what he could find out about Sam and what he was up to.

Jack sat back in his chair and flipped through his mail, and he noticed an eleven-by-fourteen manila envelope. Examining the envelope, he noted it had no return address. The post stamp was from a few towns over. He took the letter opener and slit open the envelope. He pulled out a white sheet of paper with block lettering: "STAY AWAY FROM HER OR SOMEONE WILL GET HURT."

Jack rubbed the back of his neck. *What are the odds that Sandy tells him about her disturbed ex and he gets a threatening note?* Sandy was the only woman he'd been seeing. He'd send the note for fingerprinting to see if there were any evidence on it. *Boy, this day just keeps getting better and better*, he thought. For now, he'd keep this to himself. There was no need to worry Sandy when he had no proof that the note was from Sam. *Yes, I'll check out what Sam has been up to these past few weeks*, he thought as he sat back in his chair and sighed.

14

"Sara, thanks for coming over," Wynter said as she closed the door behind Sara.

"Not a problem, kiddo."

"I picked up some Chinese. I know how you love lo mein," said Wynter.

Sara smiled. "Indeed I do."

"I brought some pinot noir. You want a glass?"

"Sounds good to me. I could use a little relaxation," Sara said as both Wynter and Sara walked into the kitchen.

Wynter poured two classes of wine and handed one to Sara. "Let's eat while it is still hot."

Both sat down at the kitchen table and started opening up the boxes of Chinese food. "Oh, let me get us some forks." Wynter got up, walked to the utensil drawer, and pulled out two forks.

"You know I love to be plied with good Chinese and

wine. So why don't you tell me what's going on?" Sara asked with a knowing look in her eye.

Wynter sat back down and handed Sara a fork. She took a sip of her wine and fingered the scar on her cheek. "Rafe broke up with me last night."

Sara put down her glass. "Aw, honey, what happened?"

Wynter pushed around her food. "Rafe told me he has a gift. He said he's a dream walker and that he killed his father through a dream. That he can't see me anymore because he won't take the risk of hurting or killing me through a dream."

"Hmm, I never heard of anyone being able to kill another through a dream," Sara said.

Wynter snorted. "Right, so what … is Rafe just using his gift as a way to break up with me? I don't understand it. Everything seemed to be going so well." Wynter sat back in her chair. "He entered into one of my vision dreams. I think that is the real reason he broke up with me. I have not met one man who can handle my gift, and now I get these weird and disturbing vision dreams." Wynter sighed. "I thought … I mean, I let myself believe that because he was my dream man that things would be different, but—"

Sara gave Wynter a sharp look. "Tell me what happened when Rafe entered your vision dream. Hmmm, vision dream, so now you have a name for this new aspect of your gift. So tell me what happened in this vision dream?"

Wynter shrugged and ran her finger around the rim of her glass. "Well, I was having one of those vague dreams, where I know something horrible is going to happen but the details are hidden from me. I was trying to see more when Rafe entered the vision. It is always so cold in those damn vision dreams, but Rafe pulled me into a hug and warmed me up. He even pulled me out of the vision dream. I mean, nothing really happened, and then he was so understanding afterward. He made me tea, and then bam! Something went off, and he pulled away and then said he couldn't see me anymore." Wynter shrugged again. "I … I just really don't know what happened. Maybe it's just me. I'm cursed or something when it comes to men."

Sara rolled her eyes. "Wynter, you can't think like that. There is nothing wrong with you. There seems to be some deep-seeded issues that Rafe is dealing with. Give him a chance, honey. He's your dream man. Let him sort out his feelings."

Wynter rubbed her scar. "That's what Gabby said when she visited me today. I guess there is also added pressure as their grandfather is in town. I know there is bad blood between Rafe and his grandfather."

Sara nodded. "Give it time. I have a feeling that things will work."

"I wish I could believe that," Wynter said with a sigh.

Sara reached out and held Wynter's hand. "Honey, please stay open. Don't close Rafe out. I have to be back in DC in the morning, but I'll be back in a few days. Just promise me you'll call me if you need to talk."

Wynter squeezed Sara's hand. "I will. I promise."

Wynter cuddled up with Rufus as they gazed at the night sky on the back porch. How she hated her vision dreams. It was bad enough with blanking out in order to find a lost item. These vision dreams were quickly becoming the bane of her existence. Despite what Sara and Gabby said, Wynter knew deep down that Rafe just could not accept her gift.

※

The next morning, Rafe pulled up in front of Wynter's house. He stared at the house, wondering how he could make things right between the two of them. *God, if only I hadn't refused the help my grandfather offered when I entered my father's dream.* He was still reeling from what his grandfather had told him. *How could my father be so cruel as to force him to watch him kill himself?* Rafe ran a hand through his hair. Just sitting here in the car certainly wasn't going to fix things between him and Wynter. He couldn't believe what an ass he'd been.

※

Wynter peeked outside her window. *Why is Rafe just sitting in his car?* Her heart hurt so much. Wynter wondered if she should give Rafe another chance. *But what if he just finds another excuse when I have another vision dream and he runs off again? Could I really stand to go through that again? God, why doesn't he just get out of his car?*

※

Rafe finally got out of his Jeep and took a deep breath before he walked up the pathway to Wynter's front door. Before he could knock, the door opened, and there stood Wynter, dressed in a black pencil skirt and white blouse. Her hair was piled in a messy knot. Stray curls framed her face. She looked beautiful.

Rafe felt his body tighten with desire. After one look from those deep blue eyes, he was hard as a rock.

"Hey, you got a minute to talk?" he asked as he shifted, trying to cover his erection.

"I'm running late for an appointment with my agent. Now is not a good time to talk." Wynter blushed, and her stomach fluttered.

"I need to explain—" Rafe ran his hand through his hair.

"Explain what? You used your father's death as an excuse to break up with me. Just admit it. You shared my vision, and it freaked you out. So you've decided that you don't need to waste your time with a woman who has freaky visions. Look, I understand. You are not the first man in my life who has run the other way when they realized what a freak I am, and I'm sure you won't be the last. Look, I'm sorry, but I really can't talk about this right now." Wynter turned to go back into the house.

Rafe grabbed her arm. "Hey, I may have freaked out when I shared your vision dream, but it had nothing to do with being in your vision dream or the vision dream itself. I had a bad experience when I was a kid, and I truly believed I killed my father. I am not your stepfather or any other man who turned away from you because of your gift. Don't judge me because of their actions. I had a long talk with my grandfather, and he explained that I could not have killed my dad."

Rafe rubbed his brow. "Look. I can see that now is not a good time to talk, but, Wynter, I've … I've fallen in love with you, and I want to make this work between us. All I'm asking is for you to give us another chance."

※

Wynter's mouth dropped open. Rafe loved her. *Oh God, I cannot deal with this right now.*

"Rafe, I … I really can't talk now," Wynter stammered.

Rafe rubbed Wynter's arm. "All right. How about I come back later tonight and we talk then?"

Wynter nodded. "Yes, tonight. We'll talk tonight."

Rafe pulled Wynter in close to him and gave her a lingering kiss. "We'll figure this out, Wynter. Just give me … give us another chance. I'll see you tonight, okay?"

Wynter nodded, worrying her bottom lip as she watched Rafe walk to his Jeep.

※

Wynter looked at her watch and realized that she would never make it back in time to meet Rafe. She looked up at Madelyn, her agent.

"Excuse me, Madelyn, but I have to make a phone call. Our meeting is taking longer than I had anticipated."

Madelyn smiled and looked serene with her dark brown hair and deep brown eyes. "No problem. I need to make a phone call myself. Why don't we take a little break and meet back here in, say, ten minutes?"

Wynter returned her smile. "Thanks. It really shouldn't take me too long." Wynter walked out of Madelyn's office and called Rafe, getting his voice mail. "Hey, Rafe, it's me. I'm sorry, but I'm tied up in a meeting with my agent, and I don't know when we'll be done. Can we reschedule for tomorrow? I really want to talk things through. It's just that this is really bad timing. Look, I gotta get back to my meeting. Okay, I'll see you tomorrow."

Wynter leaned against the wall and blew out a breath. *Yes*, she thought, *Rafe is worth fighting my fears for.*

❦

Rafe stared at his grandfather in disbelief. "I still can't believe I didn't kill my father," Rafe said as he ran his hand across his face. "He made me watch him kill himself. Why?"

Joseph sighed. "Your father had a very dark and cruel nature. I doubt that we will ever understand your father's actions."

Rafe looked at his grandfather. "You said Wynter is in danger. What danger? You really didn't go into any details before."

Joseph frowned. "I have not walked Wynter's dreams. As you know, I have a slight gift for foresight. I know that some dangerous men are after her, but I can tell you little else. One man wants to make her pay. He craves revenge against her. I believe that the only way to save your Wynter will be through your dream connection. For once, Rafael, listen to me. You need to stop fighting your gift and start embracing it. You must feel the connection between you. It will be this connection that will save her. Please let me guide you in this."

Joseph held up his hand. "I know I let you down in the past. Please don't let that color your decision now. I can help you with this."

Rafe stared at his grandfather. A frown marred his brow. "This is a lot to take in, Grandfather. I mean, for all these years, I believed I killed my father. And now you tell me that I didn't and I have wasted all this time feeling guilty and so afraid to dream walk. But now, not only do I have to accept that I did not kill my father, the sadistic bastard, for whatever reason, forced me to watch him kill himself. Not only that, now I need to know how to control my dream walking because if I don't … what … what happens to Wynter if I don't connect to my gift?"

Joseph didn't answer. He just shook his head.

Rafe grabbed his cell phone and called Wynter's cell again. The call went to voice mail. "Wynter, it's Rafe. I need to see you. Please call me. I don't care how late it is." Rafe took out his wallet and took out Jack's card.

He quickly dialed his number. "Hi, Sally. This is Rafe Wolf. Is Jack in?" Rafe sighed as he waited for Jack. "Jack, do you know where Wynter is? Yeah, Jack. Wynter and I need to work things out, but we can't do that if I can't get in touch with her. I really need to talk to her, Jack. Jack, please I'm begging you. Please tell me where she is. Jack … damn, he hung up on me," Rafe said as he threw his cell phone down on the table.

"Grandfather, I got to go. I need to find Wynter. We'll talk later, okay?" Rafe said as he rushed out of the house.

"Rafael, wait. Damn kid. He never listens."

Joseph stood up and rubbed the back of his neck. *Might as well make coffee. It will be a while before the kid gets back*, he thought with a sigh.

❀

Rafe pulled into Wynter's driveway. *Damn, her car isn't here. Where the hell could she be?* he thought.

His cell phone started to ring. He reached for it and answered on the third ring. "Wolf here. God, Wynter, where are you? I've been calling you all night. We really need to talk. I'm glad Jack told you I called. I didn't think he would. No, I didn't get your message. When will you be home? I thought you met with the author today. Oh, right, your agent. How long will you be in New York? Okay, please, sweetheart. Call me when you get back. I … yes, we really need to talk. I … I love you, Wynter. I know we can work things out. Okay, I'll wait for your call."

Rafe disconnected the call and sighed. He really wanted to get things settled between them.

❀

A few days later, Sara was staring at the crime board. She looked at the open files on the conference table and rubbed her eyebrow, trying to relieve her headache. Tapping her pen on the table, she stared at the pictures of Oscar Stanley, his deceased brother Louis, and Joey Delgado, Oscar's right-hand man, that were all up on the board. These men were definitely connected to two kidnappings, the Richards kidnapping in Black Falls and the Clark kidnapping in Point Pleasant, two seashore towns that had a huge tourist population in the summer.

Why hit the towns out of season? she thought.

She ran a hand through her curls and looked again at the files before her. Oscar and his gang were suspects in other kidnappings, but in those cases, there was no physical evidence linking them to the crimes. Brandon Clark was still missing. Iris Richards was found because her cousin Wynter had a gift for finding the missing.

Sara knew she was missing something. She raised her arms over her head and stretched, trying to ease the pain in her neck. There was a connection, but she just didn't have all the pieces yet.

A couple of years ago, Oscar and his crew were small-time crooks, but now they were masterminding a major kidnapping and human trafficking ring. Sara snorted. She didn't think so. They got away with countless kidnappings, leaving no evidence, but all of sudden, DNA was found at two crime scenes. No, someone else was the mastermind behind these kidnappings. Oscar was a follower, not a leader.

He had to be taking orders from someone else. Sara's gift was warning her that Wynter was the key to figuring out who the big boss was. She sighed in frustration as her gift for seeing connections was failing her. Feeling tense, she shrugged out of her dark blue suit jacket and put it on the back of her chair. She rolled up the sleeves of her white shirt and sighed.

Making sense out of chaos and solving puzzles was what she excelled at. But she hit a wall in this case. Sara went to the board and stared at it for several minutes.

Finally she rearranged the suspects, putting a question mark in the middle and writing "boss" under the question mark. She stepped back, satisfied with the change, knowing she was on the right track. A small smile curved her lips.

Derek Steele walked into the conference room and gave the woman standing before the crime board an appreciative glance. *Nice curves*, he thought. *Not skin and bones like so many women thought looked good.*

Steele frowned at the crime board. "You want to tell me why you rearranged my crime board, Johnson?"

Sara looked at Steele with a frown. She ran a hand through her dark curly hair, trying to tame her curls. "I don't believe that Oscar is the mastermind behind these crimes. A couple of years ago, he and his buddies were small-time operators, and now they are pulling off multimillion-dollar crimes? I just don't believe it. No, Oscar is a follower, and he is taking orders from someone else."

"Why do you have your cousin's picture on the board?" Derek asked.

Sara rubbed her brown hair. "Ah, I think there is a connection."

Derek snorted. "A connection? Are you nuts? What connection could there be between your cousin and Stanley?"

Sara closed her eyes in frustration. Then she sighed. It was never easy explaining her gift. Wynter was key in the Richards case and the reason Louis Stanley was caught.

"It's hard to explain, but I have a gift for sensing connections and solving puzzles. Wynter started Stanley's bad run with the kidnappings. If not for her, Iris Richards probably would have disappeared just like all the others. But she found Iris, and Louis Stanley was caught. I don't know yet how she fits into it all, but there is definitely a connection, and I think it is deeper than what we know now."

Steele looked at the board again. He shook his head and laughed. "A gift? Look, I've heard rumors about you, and I just want to tell you that I don't believe in that hocus-pocus shit. Just do your job and find me evidence that I can use instead of wild speculations."

Sara turned to face Steele and threw down her pen. She watched as it bounced onto the floor and shook her head. "That is exactly what I am doing. I am looking at the crime board, analyzing the evidence and seeing where it leads, and right now the evidence says that Stanley is not the leader of the crime ring. Wynter is connected, even if it is just because she found Iris Richards before she could disappear. We now have DNA from two crime scenes. It seems that Oscar is unraveling, and I feel his time is running out. He is making mistakes, and whoever the ringleader is, well, I'm sure he is not going to tolerate Oscar and his crew for much longer."

Steele spread out his hands with a shrug. "Okay, okay. Calm down, Sara. I agree. Oscar Stanley is not smart enough to run an operation like this. He is unraveling, and we might be able to use that to our advantage. Maybe he will be able to lead us to his boss. We have people watching him. All we can do now is wait for him to make his next move."

Steele put his hands in his pants pockets. "Look, I

haven't eaten since this morning. Why don't we grab a bite to eat? We have been at this for hours. We'll refuel. Maybe a break will give us a new perspective."

Sara felt herself blush. Her heartbeat quickened. "Sure, I could eat."

Sara turned to grab her jacket. Steele gazed appreciatively at her backside. *The woman certainly is built*, he thought as he took in her blue-black curls and heart-shaped face. Giving himself a mental shake, he gestured for Sara to walk out the door before him.

❦

Charles Randal was looking at a file on his desk. He glanced up at his secretary. "Silvie, make sure I'm not disturbed for the next half hour."

"Sure, Charles," Silvie said. "I'll get this letter done right away." Silvie stood up and left the office, closing the door behind her.

Charles slid his keys from his pocket and unlocked the bottom drawer of his desk. He pulled out a burner phone. He stared at it. *Damn my cousin*, he thought. He still couldn't believe he allowed himself to be set up like that. Now his cousin had photos of him at the BDSM club. Sighing, he punched in the number he had memorized.

"Yeah, it's me. I just got confirmation that DNA placed Stanley at the kidnapping site in Point Pleasant. Your boy is out of control. He's going down, my friend, and it better not link back to me. I set your guy up with Thorpe, and you assured me nothing would go wrong. You know I'm running for governor next election. Take care of this mess." Charles disconnected the call and threw the burner phone in his bottom drawer.

What a mess, he thought.

🌸

The boss leaned back in his chair. A slight frown marred his brow. He looked at the big man sitting across from him. "It's confirmed. Oscar left DNA at the Point Pleasant scene. What the hell is going on with him? I need you to find out how far his betrayal goes."

The big man smiled.

🌸

Roger Thorpe was at his garage, replacing the brakes on a Toyota Camry, when the bell rang, announcing the arrival of a customer. He put down his tool, took a dirty rag from his back pocket, and started to wipe the grease from his hands when Joey walked into the garage.

Recognizing him, he looked around the garage and shoved the rag into his back pocket. "So what are you doing here? What if someone sees you?"

Joey snorted and gave Roger a cocky smile. "Whadda you think I'm doing here? The boss wants another kid."

Roger looked up at Joey and ran a hand through his hair. "Look, man, last time was a one-time deal. There's no way I'm finding you another kid."

Joey hocked up phlegm and spit on the floor. He grabbed Roger by his shirt. "Yeah, you will. You don't want that pretty little wife of yours getting hurt now, do ya? Besides, the boss is still pissed that the last job you set up went to shit. He can't figure out how the cops found that little girl."

Roger wiped the sweat off his face. "Take it easy, Joey," he said, tugging at Joey's hands. "Now you leave my wife out of this. She's got nothing to do with this."

Joey threw him back against the counter. "Because of you and that job you set up, well, the boss is breaking my balls. Now you better find me another kid, or your wife is dead. You better find out what went wrong at that last job, ya hear me?"

Roger put up his hands. "Yeah, Joey, I hear you. As for that kid being found …" He shrugged. "Well, the sheriff's got a cousin who finds things. She found the kid."

Roger reached into his shirt pocket for his cigarettes. "Look, man, about finding another kid …"

Joey pulled a knife from his boot. "Look, jackass. You will get another kid. If you don't, well, you can say goodbye to your little wife. Now tell me about this bitch who found the kid."

Roger's hand trembled as he fumbled, trying to pull a cigarette from the pack. "Like I told you, the sheriff's cousin, Wynter, found the kid. My brother-in-law is a deputy at the sheriff's office, and he was kind of freaked how Wynter was able to locate the kid."

Joey laughed. "What the fuck you mean? What? She some kind of psychic?" He snorted.

"Well, yeah, that's it exactly. She can find things that are like lost," Roger said with a shrug. He lit his cigarette, taking a deep pull.

"No fucking way, man. Are you bullshitting me, man?"

Roger blew out smoke. "I'm telling you that she finds things. Her whole family can do stuff like that."

"No shit. Wait till I tell the boss."

"Hey now! Why do you need to tell him about Wynter? You're not gonna hurt her, are you?"

Joey poked Roger in the chest with his knife, drawing blood. "It's not your business. Your business is finding us another kid." Joey put his knife back in his boot. "You got a couple of days. Don't blow it, or you'll regret it. Got it, man?"

Roger wiped the sweat from his brow. "No, man, I don't. I'll get you what you need, just give me a couple of days."

※

Joey walked back to his truck, got in, and pulled out his cell phone. "Hey, boss. Yeah, I found the bitch who fucked up that job in Black Falls. Yeah, some chick named Wynter. She's the sheriff's cousin. Yeah, I'll find her."

※

Sara changed the station again on the radio as she drove to her mother's house. She was getting nowhere quick with the kidnapping cases. She pulled into the driveway and parked her car. She fisted her hands and hit the steering wheel. Yes, they had Oscar Stanley, but she knew they were still missing pieces of the puzzle. She knew deep down that Oscar and his crew would not lead to the mastermind behind the kidnappings.

She grabbed her jacket and got out of the car. She

stood still for a moment, breathing in deeply, trying to calm herself. She shook her head. She couldn't stop thinking that Wynter was a piece of the puzzle. But no matter how she looked at it, she couldn't figure out where that piece of the puzzle might fit.

She was not looking forward to asking her mother about Wynter's father. But it could bring her closer to connecting the dots. She just knew it. Sara sighed and slowly walked to the door.

Helen opened the door before she could knock. She gave her daughter a critical look. "God, Sara, you look like hell. I made lunch. Come in, and I'll fix you my special tea."

Besides the dark circles under her eyes, Sara looked good. Helen frowned. The weight loss concerned her.

Sara laughed. "Tell me what you really think, Mom."

"Don't sass me, missy. I see how stressed you are. So tell me what you can, and let's see if we can relieve some of your stress."

Sara smiled. Her eyes brightened. "Aw, it's good to be home." She sighed.

A warmth stole over her. It was always that way when she walked into her parents' home. She hung up her black jacket and followed her mother into the kitchen. Sara felt amusement at the differences between her and her mother. Helen was dressed in a blue tunic over yoga pants with pale pink and silver butterflies on it. Sara, on the other hand, was dressed in her standard field suit of black jacket, white shirt, and black slacks, finished off with a pair of sensible black flats.

"I could really use a cup of your special tea, Mom.

This case has me stumped. My intuition is pushing me into a rather unconventional direction. If my boss knew the direction I wanted to take this case in, he'd throw a regular hissy fit and fire my ass," Sara said with a smile.

Helen hugged Sara and brushed her hair back off her face. "Come on now. Let's go into the kitchen where you can sit down and relax for a bit. We have time enough to talk."

Sara released her hair from its tight french twist and ran her hands through her dark curls. *Yes, that feels better*, she thought.

Helen inspected her herbs, choosing the ones that would best relax and restore balance to her daughter. An aspect of her gift was being able to make a custom tea that provided a healthy balance for her clients. She put the teapot on to boil and then put the herbs and tea into a tea ball. She heated up butternut squash soup she'd made and then made a sandwich. *This should do the trick*, she thought.

The teapot whistled, and Helen poured the hot water over the tea ball and set it aside to steep. She placed a bowl of soup and the sandwich in front of her daughter. She sat across from her daughter.

"Now dig in. The tea will be ready in a minute." Helen watched her daughter take a taste of her soup. "So tell me. Do you like this new job?"

"Mmmm. God, Mom, I've missed your soups. This is delicious."

"Thanks, baby. Now tell me about your job?"

"As you know, I've been transferred. I'm now part of Derek Steele's CARD team. This case we're working on …" Sara blew out her breath. "Well, we don't have all the pieces of the puzzle, and until I find those pieces, this case is going nowhere."

Helen gave Sara a long look. She poured Sara a cup of tea. "Take a sip of this. It should help."

"Okay, okay, Mom. I love the work. It's a perfect fit for my gift. Connecting the dots and catching the bad guys. Satisfied?"

"Well, I wouldn't say satisfied, but it'll do for now." Helen took a sip of her own tea. "So what is it that you want to talk about?"

Sara pushed her hair back off her face and then grasped the mug of tea in front of her, feeling its warmth steal through her. She watched the steam rise from her cup. "I, er, want to know about Wynter's father. And before you say no, just hear me out," Sara said as she looked up at her mother.

"I know Wynter is a puzzle piece in this case. My intuition is telling me that Wynter's father is involved somehow. I know you and Aunt Brenna agreed to never talk about him, but I know this is important. This will help solve the case. This case is bigger than any of us ever thought. And please, Mom, tell me about Martin Randal."

Helen sat back in her chair. Her mouth dropped open. Whatever she thought Sara was going to ask, it certainly wasn't about Martin. Helen sighed and rubbed her neck. *Connections. First Marguerite and now Sara both asking about Martin, both in their own way, demanding answers about the past.* She always knew this day would come. *And isn't it just like Brenna to leave the mess for me to explain?*

Helen looked at her daughter. "I don't know what I can tell you."

Sara frowned. "Well, you met him. What was he like?"

Helen bit her lip and then shook her head. "He was a right bastard. When he found out Brenna was pregnant, he just left. Disappeared, like he fell off the face of the earth. Brenna was devastated."

Sara rubbed her forehead. "Is there anything else you can tell me? Do you know what happened to him?"

Helen sighed and took another sip of tea. "I don't know where he is. No one has heard from Martin since he left. He was a smooth talker, charming in a snaky way. Wherever he is, I know he probably landed on his feet. He was all about the shortcuts, scamming people. It was always so hard to imagine that Charles and Martin Randal were related. Yes, I see your surprise, but they're cousins. We tried to look for him, but maybe he's dead. Maybe he assumed a new identity. Wherever he is and whatever he's doing, I don't know about it. And quite frankly, I don't want to know. All I can tell you is that his aura was very dark, and I never got a good feeling about him. I think it was a blessing that he disappeared."

Sara stared at her mother and then closed her eyes. *God, Wynter is related to the mayor. How weird was that!* But something, some knowledge, came and went.

Sara fisted her hands in her lap. "So you think he might be living under a different name?"

"Honey, I don't have a good feeling about this. I think you should let this go. Martin always caused trouble wherever he went." Helen sighed as she saw the determined look on her daughter's face. "Aw, honey, just be careful. A lot of people can be hurt by whatever you find."

Sara shivered and rubbed her arms. "Mom, a lot of people are going to get hurt if I don't follow this lead."

Rafe sat at the kitchen table at Gabby's. He scowled down at his drink. He needed to talk with Wynter, but she got delayed in New York, meeting with one of the authors she worked with. *Damn, I have to tell her she is in danger.* But he didn't want to tell her over the phone. Hopefully they would be able to connect when she got back from her business trip. His grandfather thought time was running out.

The silver-haired man leaned back into his chair, gazing at the photo of the woman he once loved. *Brenna, darling, I can't keep my distance any longer. Our baby girl is in danger, and I will protect her. I hope you can forgive me*, he thought while tracing her face with his finger.

15

Story time at Rosie's Good Reads & Café was ending. Children were leaving the reading circle to find their parents with some running to the toy section. Rosie Thorpe had the girl-next-door look with her dark blonde hair and blue eyes. She was dressed in jeans and a green polo shirt that featured an open book with a streaming cup of coffee next to it and an apron. She looked about her store, satisfied by the turnout. It was better than last week.

She almost didn't have the heart to restart story time. Iris Richards being kidnapped from her store after story time had shocked her to her core. But as her husband Roger said, it was time to heal. Time to look to the future. Story time was one of her favorite things about owning Good Reads.

Rosie smiled sadly as she watched the kids wander around. *God, I hope I get pregnant this time*, she thought. *Lord knows how expensive the fertility treatments are.* Rosie looked up and saw Gabby Richards and Iris buying the book that was read at story time. She smiled. She was pleased to see them out and about.

"Gabby, I'm so glad to see you and Iris here today." Rosie turned to smile at Iris. "Did you enjoy today's story, Iris?"

Iris moved to stand closer to Gabby, clutching the book to her chest. Gabby put her arm about Iris's shoulders. "Yes, she loved it."

A slightly overweight woman in her late forties rushed over to Rosie and Gabby. "Rosie, I'm sorry I'm late. I've looked for Toby, but I can't find him. Do you know where he is?"

"Jenny, I'm sorry, but I haven't seen him since story time ended. A lot of the kids are in the toy section. Did you look for him there? The new Star Wars action figures just came out," Rosie said. She clasped her hands together as she slowly looked around the store for Toby. "Why don't we look together?"

Rosie glanced at Gabby. "I'm glad you came, Gabby. I hope to see you at the next story time," she said. She left with Jenny to look for Toby.

"Mommy, can we go now?" Iris asked as she looked at Roger Thorpe. "We gotta go now, Mommy."

"Okay, baby, let's buy your book, and then we'll go."

Rosie watched as Gabby and Iris left the store. Jenny Matthews came rushing toward her. Rosie put her hand on her stomach and grimaced as she thought, *Please, not again.*

"Rosie, Rosie, he's not there. Where could he be?" Jenny cried.

"Jenny, calm down. Let's look some more," Rosie said as she took Jenny's hand in hers.

Rosie looked for her husband, wondering where he went to. Always in a time of crisis, he seemed to disappear. He certainly did last year when Iris went missing, leaving her to deal with the police on her own.

※

Jack walked into Rosie's Good Reads and spotted his chief deputy, Randy Jeffers, who was trying to calm a hysterical Jenny Matthews. Randy, an older man with more gray than brown in his hair, gave Jack a weary nod as he listened to Jenny Matthews rant, "I don't understand why you are asking me these stupid questions when you should be out searching for my son! How many damn times do I have to answer these stupid questions? I told you. I was late getting here. I didn't see anything. My son is fucking missing. What are you doing to find him? He certainly isn't hiding in the bookstore."

Jack walked over and stood next to Randy. His face was set in grim lines. "Jenny, I know our questions seem stupid, but you never know what little bit of information is going to help in an investigation. An Amber Alert has gone out. My deputy, Joe Daniels, is organizing search parties. I have contacted the FBI, and a team is on its way here. I know our questions seem pointless, but believe me, the more we know, the better our chances of finding Toby are. Has Will been contacted? Is he on his way here?"

Randy turned to Jack. "I spoke with Mr. Matthews

and told him that you'd meet with him at the Matthewses' residence."

Jack sighed. "Good, good." He looked at Jenny Matthews. "Jenny, Randy will drive you home. I need to speak with Rosie, and then I'll meet with you and Will at your house. Randy will get things set up so we can trace any phone calls from the kidnapper." Jack took Jenny's hand in his. "We're doing everything we can to find Toby."

※

Jack swore in disgust as he drove over to the Matthewses' house. *Nothing. Nobody saw or heard anything. Just like in the Richards case.* Jack parked in front of the Matthewses' blue colonial house. He sat behind the wheel and slammed his hands against it. *No new leads*, he thought. As Jack walked up to the house, he called Wynter. The way things were going, he would need her help. Jenny Matthews opened the door just as Jack was finishing his call to Wynter.

"Was that your cousin you were talking to? I know you Johnsons think that you're so special. Oh, you have an ache you can't get rid of. Go see Helen. Her remedies are magic. You want something found. Go see Brenna. That's right," Jenny sneered. "I remember Wynter's mother. I know that Wynter is just like her mother. You ever think that it's your precious cousin who is behind the kidnapping? So she can play hero and suddenly know exactly where Toby is. Why aren't you interrogating her? Finding out where she took my son. Oh, I know how she found that poor girl, that Richards girl. If you ask me, your cousin is at the bottom of this. She's the kidnapper. How else would she know where to find little Iris? I want my son returned to me now and that bitch of a cousin of yours arrested for kidnapping."

A slightly overweight, balding man wearing wire-rimmed glasses, dressed in a white dress shirt and gray pants, put his arm around Jenny. "Jenny, honey, come back inside the house. You know Wynter isn't a kidnapper. She didn't take Toby."

Jenny pushed the man's arm away from her. "Don't tell me to calm down, Will. Where are the FBI? I want them to investigate our son's disappearance. You know the Johnsons are all con artists. I mean who do they think they are?"

"Jenny," Will Matthews said with a sigh. "Come back inside. The sheriff's cousin didn't kidnap Toby." Will lifted tired brown eyes to Jack. "I'm sorry, Sheriff Johnson. Please come inside. Deputy Jeffers and Deputy Daniels have everything set up to trace any calls. We're a little on edge waiting for something to happen." Will ran his hand through his thinning brown hair. "Come on, Jenny. Let Sheriff Johnson do his job."

"His job! His job! Well, let him arrest Wynter," Jenny cried.

Will walked Jenny into the living room toward the couch. "Sweetheart, I knew Wynter's mother. I don't believe that Wynter would kidnap a child in order to take credit for finding them. If your cousin Denise hadn't told you about Wynter's involvement in finding Iris Richards, then you wouldn't even know about it. Denise made a point of telling us that Wynter didn't want anyone to know about her involvement. If Wynter were really looking to take credit for finding Iris, wouldn't she want people to know about her involvement? I know Helen was unable to help your dad when he was so sick, but that doesn't mean that Wynter took our son."

Jack frowned. "Denise told you about Wynter's involvement in the Richards case?"

Jenny looked up at Jack through tear-filled eyes. "Yes, one night we were talking about UFOs and such, and Denise mentioned how she believed that some people were born with special gifts, as she saw how Wynter found that girl." Jenny wiped the tears from her face. "But what does that matter? Why haven't you found my son yet? What is being done to find my son?"

Jack sat down across from the Matthews and rubbed the back of his neck. "We have volunteers out searching. I'll be meeting with Special Agent Steele and his team. For now, there's not much else we can do. Unfortunately all we can do right now is wait to hear from the kidnappers. Deputy Chief Jeffers and Deputy Daniels will stay here with you. I am sure that someone from the FBI will want to talk with you. As soon as the FBI gets here, I'll call you."

⚜

After the long drive back from New York, Wynter headed into her bedroom and shed the suit she was wearing, changing into soft jeans and her favorite pink sweater. It was frayed along the edges, but hung loosely around her body, allowing her body to move freely. She headed into her studio and picked up her sketch pad. She wanted to get started on some of the ideas that the author she met with wanted to make to the illustrations she was working on. Wynter stared at the drawing and gave a start when her cell phone rang. Still looking at the drawing, she reached for her cell and put it on speakerphone.

"Hello?"

"Wynter, it's Jack. Special Agent Steele is meeting me at the office. Can you meet me there as well?"

Wynter rubbed her eyes. "Yeah, Jack, I'll meet you at the office."

Charles Randal sat behind his desk and loosened his tie. "Another kid has been taken from my town. Your team is out of control. Are you trying to get us caught?" he said into his burner phone. "You need to put a leash on your boy, Oscar, before he goes too far."

Charles disconnected the phone call and threw the burner phone on his desk. It was time to get out of the game. Hopefully the PI he hired to investigate Wynter Malone would give him what he needed to get out.

"Is everything set?" the man asked.

"Yeah, boss. The problem will be eliminated as planned."

The man took a sip of his coffee. The diamond on his pinky finger sparkled as the light hit it. "After this operation, I think we'll need to send a reminder to Charles of who is in charge of this outfit."

※

"I'm telling you. This Wynter chick is the one who found that little girl," Joey said as he wiped his brow.

"How did she know?" Oscar asked.

"I don't know. She's like some kind of psychic or something."

Oscar turned his chair around to face Joey. "It doesn't really matter how she did it. I want you to bring her to me. If she can work for the sheriff, then she can work for me. We'll use the kid as bait. She found the last one. She'll find this one, and we'll be waiting. Hire some extra men to watch her. Then our guys can ambush our little psychic. Because of her, my brother is dead."

※

Jack looked at his sister, who was sitting in his conference room, smirking at him. "When were you going to tell me you were part of Steele's CARD team?"

The FBI created Child Abduction Rapid Deployment (CARD) in 2005 in response to inconsistencies in response times to child abductions.

Sara gave Jack a Cheshire smile. "I'm telling you now. You know I can't talk about work."

"You could have given me a heads-up," Jack grumbled.

Sara patted Jack on his arm. "You're such a baby, Jack. Everything doesn't revolve around you."

Jack glared at Sara.

"Come on, big brother. You know I'll be an asset to the team."

"Yeah, I know. It's just—"

Sara laughed. "It's just that you're such a control freak, Jack. You think you have to be in charge of everything. I can't really see you and Steele working well together, each of you vying for the alpha position."

Jack snorted. "Yeah right! I asked Wynter to meet me here. See if we can get a jump on this thing."

Sara frowned at Jack. "I really think you and Steele need to work as a team on this, Jack. There is more going on than Toby's kidnapping."

"What aren't you telling me, Sara?"

❀

Daisy finished refilling the handsome stranger's cup of coffee. She usually didn't find men who shaved their heads attractive, but this one was hot.

"Can I get you anything else, hon?"

Sitting in the booth, the huge man grinned as he stared at Daisy's blonde hair with its lime green streaks. "No, ma'am. I'm good."

"Just let me know if you need a refill." Daisy smiled at her husband, Hank, who was staring at the stranger who was smiling at his wife.

"Yeah, I'll do that." He pulled his cell phone from his pocket and answered on the second ring. "Yeah, I'm in position. Oscar and his crew will soon be history."

❀

Wynter rushed into the sheriff's office. "Hi, Sally. I'm running late for a meeting with Jack."

"Hey, Wynter. I'll let him know that you're here."

"Thanks, Sally."

※

Roger Thorpe was at his garage under a car when the bell above the garage door rang. He slowly got up. He walked into the front room and wiped his hands on a greasy rag. Roger nodded at the big man.

"Joey was already here. I got another kid for you. What do you want?"

The big man with his shaved head smiled and pulled out a .22-caliber gun with a silencer. "I'm just cleaning up loose ends," he said as he shot Roger between the eyes. He picked up his shell casings and walked out of the garage.

※

Rafe stumbled into the kitchen, intent on getting a cup of coffee. Gabby and his grandfather were sitting at the kitchen table.

"Hey," Rafe mumbled as he walked over to the coffee machine. After pouring himself a cup of coffee, he turned toward his sister and grandfather. "Where are John and Iris?"

Gabby smiled at Rafe. "You look like shit, Rafe. But to answer your question, John and Iris are at the restaurant."

Rafe looked at his sister and glared at her. His gaze turned thoughtful when he realized that this wasn't the first time that Gabby had let Iris go with John to the restaurant without her. She was on the road to recovery, and he couldn't be more proud of her.

Joseph cleared his throat. "So Rafael, have you spoken with Wynter?"

Rafe ran his hand through his hair. "Wynter agreed to see me tonight and ... well, I guess I'm a little nervous. I didn't sleep well. Every time I closed my eyes ... well, I'd feel lost. There's a heavy weight on my chest, and then I'd wake up. I couldn't concentrate at the office, so I came home early."

Gabby looked at Rafe and ran a hand through her hair. "It seems there's been another kidnapping. Toby Matthews went missing from Good Reads earlier today. I just can't believe that it's happening again. I mean, we were there. That monster could have grabbed Iris again. I can't stop thinking about it." Suddenly she turned to the pantry and pulled out the sugar and flour.

"Isn't that the same place that Iris was taken from?" Rafe watched Gabby get eggs from the refrigerator.

"Yeah, it is. I can't believe it's happened again." Gabby shook her head in disbelief. "I almost didn't let Iris go with John, but I know how they both love spending time together in the kitchen, especially when John is trying out a new recipe. She loves being one of his taste testers."

Rafe walked over to Gabby and gave her a hug. "I'm so proud of you. You are doing so well, letting Iris go with John. I know this has to be hard on you."

Gabby turned to the counter and started measuring out the flour. "I ... well, I know that my obsessive behavior isn't doing Iris any good. I don't want to cripple her with fear."

"What time are you meeting with Wynter?" Joseph asked Rafe, hoping a change in topic would get Gabby's mind off this new kidnapping.

Rafe rubbed his neck and took a sip of his coffee. "We're going to have dinner together. Maybe my baby sister can make me some of her famous tiramisu. Wynter just loves that dessert," Rafe said with a smile.

Gabby rolled her eyes. "Well, big brother, you're in luck. I happen to have made a fresh batch of tiramisu, and yes, there is enough that you may take some with you tonight. Who am I to stand in the way of true love?" Gabby asked and then blew Rafe a kiss, her smile tired but lighter. "If you boys will excuse me, I'm running late. I'm meeting John and Iris at the restaurant. I have more baked goods to make for tonight's service." Gabby walked to the dishwasher to put her empty mug in.

After cleaning up the kitchen and putting the dough she made in a greased bowl to rise, she looked up at Rafe and her grandfather. "I'll see you two later."

"Okay, sis, thanks for the tiramisu. It just might save my relationship with Wynter," Rafe said, smiling. "I owe you one."

"Ha, you wish it was just one." Gabby pinched Rafe's cheek on her way out the backdoor.

Joseph stood up and walked to the coffee machine, refilling his mug. "So we have time to practice your meditation. You need to learn how to focus so you may enter into the dream state."

Rafe shook his head. "Granddad, I have stuff to do before I see Wynter. I don't have time to practice today."

Joseph calmly stared at Rafe. "Rafael, we don't have much time. You must practice before it's too late."

Rafe rubbed the back of his neck. "Fine. Let me finish my coffee. Then we can practice on my meditation skills."

※

Special Agent Derek Steele walked into the conference room at the sheriff's office. His smartphone was in his hand. "I got your email, Jack. Toby Matthews, Caucasian, age seven, dark blond hair, blue eyes, four foot two, weight fifty-five pounds, was taken from Rosie's Good Reads, just like the Richards girl, at approximately three thirty this afternoon. Has the forensics team found anything yet?"

"No, nothing yet," Jack said.

Sara looked up from the file she was reading and nodded. "Steele."

Steele's gray eyes flashed with impatience. "Johnson."

Wynter noticed that Steele was dressed in a dark gray suit with a white shirt and blue tie. She guessed his age to be around thirty-five. His dark brown hair was cut with military precision. Wynter stood up to introduce herself and craned her neck to look him in the eye. At six foot, he towered over Wynter.

"Hi, Special Agent Steele. I'm Wynter Malone."

Steele briefly glanced in Wynter's direction and dismissed her as he looked toward Sara. "So when is the rest of the team getting here, Johnson?"

Sara glared at Steele for the cut he gave Wynter. "They should be here within the next half hour."

"Good, good. Jack, are the parents here? I'd like to talk to them."

"They're at home. My guys are set up in case the kidnappers call."

Wynter sat back down and took a sip of water. "There are at least two kidnappers."

Steele pinned Wynter with a hard look. "Who the hell are you?"

"I … I'm Wynter," she stammered.

Steele snapped the file he had picked up closed. "I don't care what your name is. Who are you to this case? Why are you here?" he demanded.

"I … I'm Jack's cousin."

"Well, Jack's cousin, that still doesn't answer my question."

Jack held up his hand. "Enough, Steele. This is my cousin who helped us find Iris Richards."

Steele gave Wynter the once-over, taking in her faded jeans and frayed pink sweater.

"Well, well, well, so you're the psychic?" Steele snorted. "When I want my fortune read, I'll give you a call." He started toward the door and threw back over his shoulder, "Johnson, let me know when the rest of the team gets here."

16

Sara stood up and walked over to Wynter. She put her hand on her shoulder and gave her a sad smile. "Derek has a problem with psychics. He's not too happy having me assigned to his team, and I'm afraid that he took out his anger and frustrations on you."

Jack sat down next to Wynter. "Why don't you go home while Sara and I get things sorted out here at the office? Steele's still pissed off about me using you to find Iris Richards."

Wynter slumped in her chair. "Sure, call me when you need me. I think this thing will move fast."

Wynter got up and squeezed Jack's shoulder. "Don't worry so much, Jack. It'll give you more gray hair than you already have."

Jack smiled at Wynter. "Gray hair. I don't think so, cuz."

Sara watched Wynter leave and felt a chill shiver through her. *God, please protect her*, she thought.

※

Joey stood in Thorpe's garage, looking at Roger's dead body. He wiped the sweat from his forehead, pulled out his cell phone, and hit speed dial.

"Yeah, boss, we got a problem here. Thorpe's dead. Yeah, shot between the eyes. With Thorpe being dead, I don't have another contact in this town to get the extra help you wanted or find out more about that Malone chick. Yeah, sure I'll meet you there."

※

Joey stood in front of Oscar.

"So what do you have on this Malone woman?" Oscar asked.

"Ah, she's the cousin of the sheriff. I think she works from home. Thorpe really didn't say too much." Joey said as he wiped his nose on the back of his sleeve.

"Call Christopher. He's the computer whiz. Let him dig around on this Malone woman. We can't rely on the sheriff calling in his cousin to find the kid that we snatched. Tell him I want answers like yesterday, or he'll have to deal with me."

Joey pulled out his cell phone. "You got it, boss."

※

Christopher, a good-looking man in his early twenties, sat in front of a computer in a warehouse turned into an apartment. His star was definitely on the rise as a computer consultant. The phone next to him rang.

"Yeah, yeah. I got it. You want information on a Wynter Malone ASAP. I'm on it. I'll call you back in ten."

Christopher furiously typed away at his computer as he gathered intel on Wynter Malone. *Oops*, Christopher thought as he saw a red flag, indicating that one of his clients wanted to be informed of anyone doing a search on Malone.

Christopher reached for his phone and called Joey. "Yeah, I got an address right here. Yeah, she's related to the sheriff. She works from her home. Yeah, I just texted you with her address. Maybe you can catch her there."

He disconnected the call and punched in one of his biggest client's number. "Yeah, boss, I just thought you'd like to know that Joey from Oscar's crew just asked for a search regarding a Wynter Malone. Yeah, I gave him her home address … sure, boss, anytime."

Christopher sat back in his chair and smiled. That bonus would come in handy.

※

Wynter rushed to her car. Rafe was supposed to come over tonight. Maybe the timing would work out. *God, I'm running late*, she thought. *Just my luck*. She just had to work things out with him. Love was worth the risk. She unlocked the car door, opened it, and slid into the driver's seat. Her dreams flashed through her mind. She gripped the steering wheel tightly. She'd found her soul mate. He was worth the risk. She nodded her head and turned the key. *Yes*, she thought, *love is definitely worth the risk.*

※

The boss man sat back in his chair and stared at one of his daughter's pencil drawings that he was able to obtain. Oscar and his crew were a problem. They had fucked up not following orders, taking action on their own, and leaving a sloppy crime scene. But now this, Oscar and his crew were now endangering his daughter. He picked up his phone and hit a button.

"I want Oscar Stanley to suffer before he dies. Is that understood? I want you to find Wynter Malone. She is not to be hurt, understood? Call me when it's done."

※

Wynter walked into her house. She looked around and shivered at the unnatural silence. Chills crawled down her spine.

"Rufus! Hey, boy, I'm home." Wynter walked through the living room into the kitchen and found Rufus lying unconscious on the ground. She ran to him. "Rufus! Oh my God, Rufus," she said as she knelt down beside him and ran her hands lightly over him. "What's wrong, boy?"

Joey walked into the kitchen. "Nothing's wrong with your dog, lady. He's just knocked out." He wiped his nose on his sleeve.

Wynter stood up slowly. "Who the hell are you, and

what are you doing in my house? What did you do to my dog?" She moved slowly toward the counter.

Joey walked toward Wynter. "Look, lady, we can do this the easy way or the hard way. It don't matter much to me."

"What do you want?" Wynter asked again as she blindly reached for the knife on the kitchen counter.

Joey rushed toward Wynter and pushed her against the sink, away from the counter, bringing out a chloroform-soaked cloth and pushing it against her face. Wynter struggled and shoved her knee into his groin. Joey grunted and leaned harder into Wynter. The cloth firmly pressed against her nose and mouth. Wynter started to feel dizzy. Her hands flapped as she tried to hit her attacker.

"Hey, lady, whatcha do that for?" was the last thing Wynter heard as she sank into darkness.

※

Joe Daniels stood before Jack. His hands were clenched at his sides.

"Joe, I know you want to be with Rosie right now, and I don't blame you. But Toby is still missing, and I need you here. Okay, Joe?" Jack asked.

Joe rubbed his hands over his face. "Yeah, Jack, I know. But man, this is so fucked up. Rosie was devastated when Iris went missing. You know she and Roger are trying to get pregnant, right? This … well …" Joe ran his hand through his straight black hair. His brown eyes were closed.

Jack looked at Joe and slowly shook his head. He looked younger than his twenty-seven years. "Man, I didn't know. I know this is hard, but Toby has to take priority. I'm sending Denise over to the bookstore to talk with Rosie. She'll take good care of your sister. Right now Jenny and Will need you here, working to find their son."

Joe nodded and sighed hard. "Okay, Jack. Okay."

17

DEREK STEELE RAN HIS hand over his eyes and then returned to watching the surveillance tape from the bookstore again. They had nothing, not a damn thing. *No call from the kidnappers and no luck with the search party. Just nothing.* Whoever took Toby knew where the surveillance cameras were at the bookstore. There was no clear shot of him, just a guy with his head down wearing a ball cap.

Shit, Steele thought, *this has to end. All we need is one little break. Somebody has to know who this guy in the ball cap is.* Steele stood up and grabbed his jacket. He turned to Agent Fresco, who was also reviewing the surveillance tapes.

"Print me a copy of the guy wearing the ball cap. I'm gonna go back to the bookstore and see if the owner doesn't know who that guy is. I think she knows more than she's telling."

Charles Randal leaned back in his chair. He'd just finished reading the report he received from the private investigator that he hired. Wynter Malone was his cousin's daughter. He remembered Brenna Malone. She was a beautiful woman, just the kind of woman that his cousin was attracted to. This was the information he needed. There had to be a reason his cousin didn't want people knowing Wynter Malone was his daughter. *Maybe now I can get out from under my cousin's thumb and be done with this nasty business. Sure, I'll miss the money, but I have my future to think about, and my cousin's operation is falling apart. That stupid bastard Oscar certainly fucked things up.* Charles smiled. His eyes were cold. *Yes, my day is looking up,* he thought.

A knock sounded at the door, and his daughter Kimberly walked in. Kimberly looked older than her thirty-seven years. Her party lifestyle did her no favors. Her bleached blonde hair was pulled back into a french twist, and her hazel eyes held a calculating gleam as she smiled at her father. She patted her hair and then touched the diamond stud earrings her husband had given her.

Charles eyed his daughter critically and found her to be fashionably thin. He thought she didn't wear it well. She could stand to gain a few pounds.

"Hey, Daddy." Kimberly leaned down to kiss his cheek. "We need to get going if we want to make our reservations."

Silvie knocked on the door and walked in, interrupting Kimberly. "Charles, Mrs. White is here to pick up those contracts. I know you wanted to talk with her. Do you have a minute?"

Charles looked at his daughter and walked to the door of his office. "Sweetheart, give me just a minute. I won't be long. I promise we'll make our reservation."

Silvie glanced at Kimberly and then quickly followed Charles out of the office, not wanting to hear Kimberly complain.

"Dammit, every time something comes up," Kimberly muttered. "It's always something with him."

She flung herself into her father's chair and made a huffing sound. She looked at the files on his desk and saw a file with her uncle's name on it. She opened it and starting reading. A wicked smile spread across her face as she continued to read.

Oh yeah, I'll get even with those snotty Johnsons, she thought. *So the freaky deek is my second cousin.*

"How interesting," she said out loud.

Charles walked back into his office. "What's interesting, sweetheart? What are you looking at?" Charles noticed the file she was reading. He grabbed the file from Kimberly's hand. "You had no right to look at the files on my desk. How dare you." His face turned red.

Kimberly smiled. Her eyes gleamed with malicious intent. "I can't wait to tell that bitch Wynter who her daddy is."

Charles walked around his desk and pulled Kimberly up from the chair, shaking her. "You will do no such thing. You have no idea how important it is to keep this information quiet."

Shocked, Kimberly pulled away from her father. "But Daddy—"

Charles slapped her across the face. "You will listen

to me just this once, Kimberly. Grow up. Jack Johnson didn't want you in high school, so what? You are a grown woman with a wonderful husband. Douglas is a fine man and is madly in love with you. What more could you possibly want? If it gets back to me that you said anything to Wynter about your uncle." He shook her again. "And it will get back to me. I will cut you off. No more money. Do you understand me?" Charles asked roughly. "Do you?"

Kimberly angrily brushed the tears off her face. "Yes, Daddy, I understand."

※

Jack pulled in front of Thorpe's Garage. Deputy Denise Blake was crouched beside the body of Roger Thorpe, taking pictures of the crime scene. Denise looked over at Jack as he walked over to her. Denise often reminded Jack of a mini blonde Valkyrie. Many a man had underestimated her, but her small size hid a fierce fighting spirit, and her quickness put many a man on his back. Today, her hazel eyes held sorrow as she looked up at Jack.

"Shot between the eyes. Looks like a professional hit. Who would want to kill Roger? Poor Rosie, she was already devastated when he hadn't come home. She was worried that something happened to him. How do I tell a woman who had two kids snatched from her bookstore that her husband's been murdered? What the hell is going on in our town, Jack? First the kidnappings, and now this."

Jack knelt down next to Denise and looked down at the body. "Looks like a twenty-two-caliber pistol was used. What the hell was Roger into? This was definitely a hit. Is Tom on his way? I don't want to move the body until he has had a chance to examine it."

"Yeah, he should be here soon," Denise said as she slowly stood up.

Jack stood up and looked around the garage. "Could this day get any worse?" he asked with a sigh.

※

Derek Steele entered Rosie's Good Read, looking to speak with Rosie Thorpe. He spotted her by the history section, shelving books. He slowly made his way toward her, taking in her swollen red eyes.

"Mrs. Thorpe, I have a few more questions for you. Can we sit down and talk? I'm sorry to trouble you, but it could help us find Toby."

Rosie pulled a tissue from the back pocket of her jeans and blew her nose. She nodded and led him to the back office. She sat behind the desk and nodded to Steele to sit across from her. "Yes, anything to help find Toby. I just can't believe it happened again. First Iris and now Toby."

Derek took the picture from his pocket. "I have a photo I would like you to look at. It's not much, but maybe you can help me identify the picture."

Rosie took the photo from Steele and gave it a long look. "I really can't tell you who is in the photo, and that cap is popular around here. Why, even my husband has a cap like that."

Jack walked into the office, and both Steele and Rosie turned to look at him.

"Rosie," Jack said and then stopped when he noticed Derek. "Steele, what are you doing here?"

Steele looked at Jack. "Just showing Mrs. Thorpe a picture. Hoping she could identify the man in the photo. What brings you here, Johnson?"

"I need to speak to Rosie." Jack looked down at his shoes.

Rosie looked at Jack and sniffled. "What's going on, Jack?" Her hand trembled when she pulled a tissue from the box on her desk.

Jack knelt in front of Rosie and took her free hand into his. "Rosie, I have bad news. Roger, well, Roger is dead. He was shot."

Rosie's face lost all color. "But that's impossible," Rosie stammered. "I mean, did you say he was shot? Who would shoot Roger? I don't understand," Rosie cried.

Jack squeezed Rosie's hand. "I don't know, Rosie. Has Roger been acting differently lately? Did he maybe tell you he was having any problems with anyone?" Jack asked.

Rosie wiped her nose with the tissue and looked at Jack. "No, no, nothing. I just can't believe someone would hurt Roger. I mean ..." Rosie pulled her hand out of Jack's and wiped at her eyes. "I finally got pregnant, Jack. How can Roger be gone when all of our dreams are coming true? I just don't understand it."

Jack stood. "I'm gonna call Joe, Rosie. He'll bring your sister. I want you to know that we are doing everything we can to find out who killed Roger."

Jack gave Steele a sharp glance and walked over to the register to call Joe. Steele slowly made his way to Jack. Rosie's sob could be hard from the office.

"Yeah, Joe. She's pretty shaken. The sooner you get here, the better. Yes, I'll stay with her until you get here." Jack disconnected the call and eyed Steele. "So who is the guy in the photo?"

Steele rubbed the back of his neck. "I have no positive ID, but I think it's Thorpe. Mrs. Thorpe confirmed that her husband has the same cap as the guy in the photo. So Thorpe is dead?"

"Yeah, shot between the eyes. Twenty-two caliber. Professional hit," Jack said, keeping an eye on Rosie. "Why don't you grab us some coffee and a cup of tea for Rosie from the café? I'll stay with her. After Joe gets here, we'll talk."

※

Jack was driving back to his office. His cell phone rang, and he pulled it off the clip to answer.

"Johnson here. Sara? Sara, calm down. What? Wynter. What about Wynter? All right. I'll drive to her place and call you when I get there."

Jack disconnected the call and did a U-turn. He sped to Wynter's house. As he pulled into the driveway, he noticed the house was in complete darkness, which was not normal for Wynter. The door was unlocked.

Jack called out, "Wynter, are you here? Rufus, where are you, buddy?" Jack walked through the living room into the kitchen and saw Rufus lying on the kitchen floor.

He rushed to Rufus, who whined when he felt Jack rub his ear. "Hey, buddy, who did this to you? Where's Wynter?"

Jack pulled out his cell phone and called Sara. "She's gone. Rufus has been hurt. I'll take him over to the vet. Call Denise and see if she is finished at Thorpe's Garage. I need her to come here and start processing this crime scene. Christ, what's going on here, Sara? Also, let Steele know that Wynter is missing. And Sara, stop blaming yourself. You know you can't always stop bad things from happening. I'll meet you back at the office after I drop off Rufus."

Jack disconnected the call and paused as he heard a car pull into the driveway. Jack stood up slowly and pulled his gun from its holster as he walked toward the front door. Peering out the window, he saw Rafe get out of his SUV. He quickly holstered his gun and opened the door before Rafe could knock.

"Hey, Rafe. Look, man, I got to take Rufus to the vet's. Wynter is missing, and one of my deputies is on the way here." Jack looked at Rafe. "Hey, I have an idea. Would you take Rufus to the vet's. Give my mother a call, and she'll call Dr. Spakler, who can meet you at her office. I would really appreciate it."

Rafe stood frozen by the front door. "What happened? Wynter and I were supposed to meet for dinner." Rafe ran his hand through his hair. "Did you say Wynter is missing? Rufus is hurt? What's going on, Jack?"

Jack pushed past Rafe and walked back into the house toward the kitchen. "Look, I don't have time to explain." Jack walked into Wynter's kitchen, looked at Rufus, and then peered at Rafe, who had followed behind him.

"Hey, give me a hand with Rufus." They picked up Rufus and walked back out, bringing Rufus to Rafe's

SUV. Rafe struggled to open the backdoor of the SUV and keep a grip on Rufus. Once he managed to open the door, he and Jack placed Rufus gently on the seat.

"You'll be all right, buddy. Rafe here is going to take you to the doctor," Jack said as he rubbed Rufus's head.

Rafe closed the backdoor and looked at Jack. "What happened here? What do you mean Wynter is missing? I … Wynter and I were supposed to talk. God, what happened?" Rafe asked, shocked that Wynter was missing.

Jack rubbed the back of his neck. "This day has just taken a turn for the worse. Sara knew something was wrong, but what with the Matthews boy missing and Thorpe's death, there just wasn't enough time to check in with Wynter. I don't know what happened, but I do know that my cousin wouldn't leave Rufus when he was hurt. Look, I don't really have time right now, but when I know something, I'll give you a call. Please just take care of Rufus, and I'll start the search for Wynter," Jack said as he turned to go back into Wynter's house, leaving a shocked Rafe to take care of Wynter's dog.

Rafe got into his truck, pulled out his cell phone, and called Helen. "Yeah, Helen, it's Rafe. Wynter is missing. I have Rufus, who is hurt. I need directions to Dr. Spakler's office. Jack is processing Wynter's house for clues. I don't really know what happened. I need to get Rufus to the vet's. Please give me directions. What? I don't know, Helen. Just please give me directions. I will call you as soon as I know anything, but I'm sure Jack will be calling you. Yeah, got it. Thanks, Helen."

Rafe disconnected the call and stepped on the gas. He needed to get this done so he could get back to Gabby's and his grandfather. There just had to be something he could do.

❧

Joseph Wolf took down a mug from the kitchen cabinet. "Rafael, you need to relax. You must tap into your dream walking abilities," Joseph said.

Rafe looked at his grandfather and rubbed his tired eyes. "Wynter is missing. I walked out on her, and we never got a chance to clear the air between us." Rafe shook his head. "I didn't get the chance to make things right between us. I didn't get to tell her how much I love her, and now she is missing. How am I supposed to relax and dream walk?"

Joseph looked at Rafe across the kitchen table. "If ever there were a time to listen to me, now is that time. I have prepared a calming tea that will help you relax. You must use your connection to Wynter, if you are to find her. Time is running out," Joseph said. He poured the tea into the mug and handed Rafe the cup filled with his calming brew.

Rafe took the mug from his grandfather. "This had better work, Grandfather." Rafe downed the tea, grimacing at the bitter taste.

Joseph stood and took the empty mug from Rafe. "I suggest you lie down and let the brew work its magic. Take deep, calming breaths."

Rafe stood and turned to go to his room. "I hope this works."

"Go. I will watch over you."

Rafe walked down the hallway to his bedroom at his sister's house. *God, I miss you, Wynter,* Rafe thought as he stretched out onto his bed. *This has to work* was his last thought as his body relaxed into sleep.

Rafe slowly became aware of being in a bookstore. Fairies danced around colorful stuffed animals. Huge butterflies flew in front of him. Ahead, he saw a little girl sitting at the feet of a princess who was waving her wand. As he drew nearer, he recognized his niece Iris.

Rafe walked over to where Iris was and sat down next to her on the floor. "What's up, kiddo?"

Iris turned to look at Rafe. "The story's about to end. Then the bad part starts," Iris whispered.

"Bad part. What bad part?" Rafe asked as he realized he was dream walking in Iris's dream.

"When the bad man takes me, like what happened with Toby," Iris said as she put a curly lock of her black hair in her mouth.

Rafe looked down at Iris. "You know the man who took Toby?"

Iris clutched Rafe's hand. Her face scrunched up. "No, no! I don't want to see, Uncle Rafe."

Rafe sat down next to Iris, pulled her onto his lap, and stroked her hair. "Iris sweetie, I'm here with you. Maybe together we can see the man who took you and took Toby today. He can't hurt you here, not with me here. Do you think you can look and see who the bad man is?"

Iris hugged Rafe, hiding her face into his neck. "I'll try, Uncle Rafe. Promise me you won't leave me?"

"I promise, Iris. You just lead the way. I'll be right next to you."

Suddenly the scene changed. Screeching flying monkeys were flying toward them, and a distant figure started toward them. Rafe and Iris walked slowly as the flying monkeys swooped in front of them as they drew nearer to the man at the end of the hall. Thunder crashed, and an eerie green lightning lit the sky.

"Iris, do you remember your drawing that you showed me when I first arrived at your house?"

Iris looked up at Rafe. "Yes."

"Why don't you bring the unicorn here? Just picture him in your mind and wish him here. Do you think you can do that?"

Iris frowned but nodded. "Yes, I think I can do that," she said as she closed her eyes really tight and thought of Stanley, her magic unicorn. Suddenly a beautiful unicorn, with the colors of the rainbow, appeared.

Iris opened her eyes and clapped her hands together. "Look, Uncle Rafe. I did it. Stanley's here. Isn't he beautiful?" she whispered as she twirled in a circle.

"Yes, he is certainly beautiful. Stanley huh! Well, Stanley we have a bit of a problem and need your help. Can you stop the thunder and lightning and make the monkeys disappear?"

Stanley danced around, and all the colors of the rainbow flew into the air. And just like that, the monkeys disappeared, and the thunder and lightning stopped.

"Great job, Stanley!" Iris cried.

A beautiful rainbow appeared in the sky.

"Whoa! Uncle Rafe, look at the rainbow. Isn't it beautiful?"

Rafe stood amazed at the sight of the rainbow. The colors just glowed.

"Iris, what a beautiful rainbow you and Stanley created. You did a great job, kid. Now let's look at the bad man. He's just an ordinary guy who can't hurt you here. Look at the magic that you and Stanley produced. You can do this too, Iris, okay?"

Iris gripped Rafe's hand harder and swallowed. "Okay, Uncle Rafe. With you and Stanley here, I know I can do this."

Slowly the man's features became clearer. A sense of familiarity came over Rafe as he watched the man's features come into focus.

"I think I know this guy," Rafe said as he searched his mind, trying to place where he knew this guy from. "I think that guy is Wynter's mechanic."

Iris nodded. "He's Miss Rosie's husband," Iris whispered.

In that second, Rafe sat up and hit his head against the headboard of his bed. Leaning forward, he rubbed the back of his head and winced. Turning his head, he saw his grandfather sitting in a chair next to his bed.

"Grandfather, oh my God, I just dream-walked in Iris's dream. She remembered who took her from Rosie's Good Reads. It was Rosie's husband. My God! We've got to call Jack. This could be a lead in finding Wynter."

Joseph leaned forward and touched Rafe's arm. "Calm down, Rafael. First let us check on Iris. She is awake and will need us to help her explain things to her parents."

"Iris's dream was amazing, Grandfather. She brought a unicorn she drew into her dream. It was just amazing.

The colors were fantastic. She was fantastic," Rafe said as he jumped out of bed to go to Iris's room, down the hall from his.

Iris stood in the doorway of her room, and when she saw Rafe, she ran into his arms. "Uncle Rafe, we did it! I remembered who the bad man was. Stanley was just so beautiful, don't you think, Uncle Rafe?"

Rafe hugged Iris to him. "Slow down, Iris. Yes, Stanley was beautiful. I'm so proud of you. You faced your fear. Your dreams should start to get better, and now you know that Stanley can visit you in your dreams. You took control," Rafe said as he spun Iris around in a circle.

Gabby and John came down the hall to see Rafe with a giggling Iris and Joseph smiling at them.

"What's going on here? You guys having a party and didn't invite us?" Gabby asked as she tied the belt of her robe.

Iris wiggled out of Rafe's arms and ran to her mother. "Mommy, I remembered. I remembered who the bad man was! Uncle Rafe and Stanley helped me remember, and it was beautiful. Stanley made beautiful rainbows, and Uncle Rafe was there with me."

Gabby glanced at Rafe. "Slow down, Iris. You remembered the bad man?"

Iris nodded. "Yeah, it was Miss Rosie's husband. He was the one who took me to the other bad men. I don't remember how I got there." Iris pulled at her mother's robe. "Is that okay, Mommy? That I don't remember that part?"

Gabby hugged Iris to her. "Of course, honey. It's fine."

Iris grinned at her mother. "We couldn't have done it without Stanley, right, Uncle Rafe?"

Rafe smiled at his niece. "Right, Stanley really pulled through for us, Iris."

John reached out and tugged on Iris's curls. "Who's Stanley, sunshine?"

Iris yawned and leaned into her father. "He's the unicorn I drew at Wynter's. He was so beautiful, Daddy. I wish you could have seen him."

John leaned down and kissed Iris on the forehead. "I do too, sunshine. It sounds like you and Uncle Rafe had quite the adventure."

Iris yawned again. "Yes, an adventure."

Gabby looked at John. "I'll put Iris back to bed. I think Uncle Rafe has some explaining to do. Why don't you make us coffee and I'll be there in a few minutes?"

John looked at his wife and daughter and smiled. He had a feeling their life was about to take a turn for the better. "Yes, that sounds like a good idea."

❧

Rafe, Gabby, John, and Joseph sat around the kitchen table. Gabby had both hands wrapped around her mug. "Okay, Rafe, what the hell happened with you and my daughter?"

Rafe looked at Joseph, who nodded to him. "Gabby, it was incredible! Grandfather gave me a tea, and when I fell asleep, I was in Iris's dream. At first she was scared because she knew the bad man was coming for her, but I told her that I was with her and then suggested she bring

Stanley into the dream and then ..." Rafe gestured with his hands. "Poof! There were rainbows and a dancing unicorn who took away Iris's fear. Then suddenly the man's face became recognizable, and it was Wynter's mechanic. Do you realize the power that Iris has, Gabby? She manifested Stanley in her dream. She changed her dream. It was ... I don't know ... the only word that comes to mind is *amazing*!" Rafe said with a laugh.

Gabby glared at Rafe. "What are you telling me, Rafe, that Iris can dream walk? That she's like you? How can you be sitting there smiling when you have denied your dream walking?" Gabby used air quotes. "Abilities for as long as I can remember? Do you think I want that for Iris? How is that a good thing?"

Rafe reached over and took Gabby's hand into his. "Gabby, I was wrong to run away from my gift. I can see that now."

John looked at his wife. "What the hell are you talking about? What the hell is dream walking, and why is this the first time I'm hearing about it?"

Gabby shrugged her shoulders. "It's Rafe's gift from Grandfather. I never thought ... I mean, it just never occurred to me that I could pass on the gift to Iris," Gabby said as she looked at her grandfather. "Why didn't I know that I could pass on the family gift? All I remember is that it was supposed to pass down from father to son. So how is it possible that Iris has this *supposed* gift?"

Joseph looked at Gabby and shrugged. "Your father is the one who spouted that nonsense. You children never listened to me. If you had, you would have known that you could pass this gift onto your daughter."

John shook his head. "So what you're telling me is that Rafe and Iris both have this dream walking gift and that what? I really don't understand what happened tonight with my daughter."

Rafe took a sip of his coffee. "Well, tonight I was trying to connect with Wynter, but instead I ended up in Iris's dream. I'm no psychologist, but I think tonight was a big breakthrough for Iris. I was able to help Iris face her fear, and she was able to remember the man who took her from the bookstore. She brought the unicorn from her drawing into her dream. He helped her conquer her fear and allowed her to see the face of Wynter's mechanic."

Rafe smiled as he looked down at his coffee cup. "It was amazing. The colors! Just amazing!" Rafe looked at John. "Your daughter turned her nightmare into a world of beauty where rainbows flashed in the sky."

Joseph nodded at John. "When done properly, the dream walker acts as a guide to help others take control of their dreams. Because Iris is also a dream walker, she was able to manifest the unicorn into her dream. Really! It is quite exciting. She is so young, yet she brought her drawing of a unicorn to life."

Gabby pushed away her coffee cup from her. "Hold it right there, Grandad. Iris is too young for this gift or whatever you want to call it. I don't want what happened to Rafe to happen to my daughter. So you can just get that smug smile off your face."

Joseph closed his eyes and then looked at Gabby. "Then don't make the same mistake that Rafael made. He ran away from his gift, and now he is struggling with it and isn't connecting with his woman as he should. Don't ignore this, Gabriella. Iris's gift is real, and she needs to be instructed on how to handle her gift."

John put his arm around Gabby. "Baby, I don't know anything about dream walking, but if your grandfather can help Iris, then I think we should let him help her with this dream walking stuff. From what Rafe has said, Iris turned her nightmare into a beautiful fantasy with her unicorn. All I know is that, when I looked at you and Iris tonight, I felt something tight and painful release within me. A hard knot unraveled within me. I know that things are going to get better. For a while there, I just … well, I felt I was losing you both, but now I really think we have a chance to turn things around."

Gabby shook her head. "Rafe … I …"

"Gabby, trust me and follow Grandfather's advice. I didn't, and now I am paying a very steep price. Wynter is missing, and I can't connect with her. She's out there, and I don't know what is happening with her, if she's hurt or worse."

A tear slid down Gabby's cheek. "I know you will connect with Wynter, Rafe. It will happen."

"Now we need to get in touch with Jack. I think this information will help him find that missing kid and Wynter," Rafe said.

※

Wynter shivered and groaned in pain. *What the hell happened?* she thought. Cracking an eye, she quickly closed it again as a wave of dizziness and nausea hit her. Her chest felt heavy, and her breathing was labored.

After a minute, she slowly opened her eyes. Her head was pounding. *Breathe, Wynter. Slow and deep*, she thought. Her heart thundered in her ears.

Wynter gingerly turned her head to see where she was. Her eyes landed on the body of a small boy lying on a mattress across the room from her. Wynter sat up quickly. Her stomach rumbled, and she put her hand to her mouth to keep from vomiting. She took a deep breath and slowly leaned against the wall.

"Toby, can you hear me? Are you all right?" she croaked.

"Wh … who are you?" Toby stuttered.

"I'm Wynter. Are you okay? Have you been hurt?"

"No," Toby whispered, "I wanna go home."

"I know, sweetie. We'll get out of here somehow. I want to go home too. I need you to stay calm for me, buddy. Do you think you can do that?"

Toby nodded.

"You are being very brave. Hey, my cousin is the sheriff, and I know he is looking for us. You're not alone anymore. We'll get through this together," Wynter said as she shook her head, trying to stay focused. She squeezed her eyes shut, waiting for the room to stop spinning.

"Do you know how we got here Toby?" she whispered.

"Mr. Thorpe," Toby sniffled. "You know, Miss Rosie's husband. He said he'd show me the new Star Wars action figures, but when we got to the back room, he grabbed me and took me outside, and this other guy took me here. He put something over my head and told me that if I didn't do as he said he'd hurt my mom," Toby cried. "He didn't hurt my mom, did he?"

Wynter crawled over to Toby and hugged him to her. "I don't know, sweetheart," Wynter said as she rocked them both back and forth, wondering how everything went to shit.

18

Jack pulled up in front of the Richardses' house, feeling a sense of déjà vu. *God, am I tired*, he thought as he walked up to the front door. Gabby opened it before he could knock.

"Hi, Jack. Come on in. Something incredible has happened. Iris remembered who initially took her. I mean, she's sleeping now, but Rafe can fill you in. He knows more about it."

Rafe put his hands on Gabby's shoulders and looked at Jack. "Hey, Jack, let's go to the kitchen, and I can tell you what has happened. You look like you could use a cup of coffee."

Gabby went and got a mug from the cabinet and poured Jack some coffee. "Do you take milk or sugar?"

Jack looked at the mug appreciatively and sighed. "No, black is fine. It's been a long day and night. So what's going on?" Jack took a seat next to John and stared at Joseph.

Rafe sat down next to his grandfather. "Jack, this is my grandfather, Joseph Wolf. Grandfather, this is Sheriff Johnson, Wynter's cousin."

Jack reached across the table to shake hands. "Nice to meet you. Sorry it's under these circumstances."

Joseph smiled and shook hands with Jack. "Yes, a pleasure in this dark time."

John leaned forward. "Okay, now that everyone knows each other, let's move on, shall we?"

Rafe nodded. "Yes, umm, did Wynter tell you about my dream walking, Jack?"

Jack shook his head. "Nah, she told Sara, who then told me, so this is about dream walking because I gotta tell you, as interesting as the topic is, I'm a little busy right now and I think this can wait."

Rafe held up his hand. "Please, Jack, just give me a minute to explain. As you may know, I kind of repressed my gift because I thought it was dangerous. But my grandfather explained some things to me, and well tonight, I dream-walked into Iris's dream. Jack, she saw who initially took her from the bookstore. It was Wynter's mechanic. Thorpe, I think his name is. Anyway, maybe he knows who took Toby and what happened to Wynter."

Jack sat back in his chair and sighed. "Thorpe, huh? Well, that explains a few things. Unfortunately Thorpe is dead. He was murdered earlier today. I guess this is what he was into and why he was killed. He isn't going to be answering anyone's questions."

Gabby gasped and leaned into John. "Poor Rosie. I

mean, first the kidnapping and now this. Does she know anything?"

Jack sighed again. "An agent is talking with her, but as it is an ongoing investigation, there really isn't much I can tell you."

Rafe frowned. "Right, I remember. You mentioned the name Thorpe, but I was focused on Wynter's disappearance. I just didn't connect it."

"Yeah, well this is good information. I'll call it in and see if Rosie knows anything about Thorpe's connection to the kidnappings." Jack stood up. "Look, I'll come around tomorrow morning and speak with Iris. Who knows? This might help in finding Toby."

Rafe looked at Jack and rubbed the back of his neck. "Any word on Wynter?"

Jack just shook his head no and left.

Rafe turned to his grandfather with his hands clenched into fists. "You have to help me, Grandfather. Give me more of that tea. Anything! I need to connect with Wynter. I've got to find her."

Joseph shook his head. "No more tonight. You must rest. Tomorrow we will work on getting your Wynter home. You have made great strides tonight. Dream walking is not something you can rush, Rafael."

John hugged Gabby to him. "He's right. We should all get some sleep. Tomorrow will come soon enough."

Rafe glared at John and his grandfather. "How can I sleep when Wynter is missing and in danger?"

Joseph gave Rafe a small smile. "I wouldn't worry about that. You've expended a lot of energy tonight, and shortly you will feel it. Anyway, something tells me that your Wynter will be found."

※

Wynter looked around. They were in a basement. She and Toby were on a musty old mattress. She stiffened when she heard footsteps on the stairs. Toby whimpered and slid closer to her. Wynter hugged him closer to her as two men came into view. One was the man who hurt Rufus and kidnapped her.

"What the fuck, Joey? I thought you said she'd be out for a few more hours."

"Fuck, man. No names, *Pete*, and yeah, she should be. Come on. Help me with the girl. We can tie her to that chair over in the corner," Joey said as he walked toward them.

Wynter tightened her hold on Toby. "No, wait. Please don't do this."

Joey reached down and backhanded her. "Shut up, bitch. If you don't want the kid hurt, you'll get your ass over to that chair." When Wynter didn't respond fast enough, Joey said with menace, "Now!"

Wynter stifled a scream and brought her hand up to her throbbing cheek. "All right. Please give me a minute. Just don't hurt Toby." Wynter struggled to get up.

Joey yanked her to her feet and dragged her over to the chair. "Go get the zip ties," Joey said to Pete. "And you, don't think I forgot you hit me in the nuts, lady. You'll pay for that. Now stop struggling."

Joey pushed her into the chair. "Come on, Pete. Where are those fucking ties? I need them now."

Pete grabbed the ties from the duffel bag he brought with him and put it on the floor next to the mattress. "I got them right here." He walked over to Joey and handed them to him.

"Good." Joey yanked Wynter's arms behind her and zip-tied her hands, pulling it tight.

"Ow, hey, not so tight. You're cutting off the circulation," Wynter cried as she struggled to get loose.

Joey backhanded her again. "Shut up, bitch." Joey knelt down in front of her and tied each leg to a chair leg.

"It's too tight."

Joey punched Wynter, knocking her unconscious. "About time you shut up, you stupid bitch."

"Hey, didn't the boss want to talk to her?" Pete turned to stare at Toby and moved his hand to rub his crotch.

Joey shrugged. "I tapped her. She'll wake soon enough. Come on. We gotta meet with Mike. Let's go."

Toby curled into a tight ball and whimpered as he heard the men leave.

❋

Jack closed the file in front of him and looked across the conference table at Steele.

"Okay, you concentrate on finding Toby, and I'll concentrate on finding Wynter. Sara believes, where we find one, we will find the other. I don't understand how Thorpe is involved in all this, but there is a connection. I have one of my men going through his financials."

"Good. I'll keep you posted if anything new comes up concerning the Matthews kid."

Steele looked Jack directly in the eye. "I'm sorry about your cousin."

Jack rubbed the back of his neck. "Thanks."

The next morning, the big man was in a black sedan, staring at a house. Its owners were on vacation. He took out his cell phone and punched in a number.

"Yeah, boss. I found Ms. Malone. Joey and Pete have her and the kid at a house. Owners are on vacation." The big man nodded. "Okay, boss, consider it done," he said and then disconnected the call as he rolled and cracked his neck.

Jack stood and stretched. Slowly he rolled his shoulders. *God, that couch is uncomfortable*, he thought, *but that's what I get for spending the night in his office.*

Thankfully he kept a change of clothes for just this type of situation. In the bathroom, off his office, he threw cold water on his face and then brushed his teeth. He ran his fingers through his damp hair. It was the best he could do. He glanced at his watch—6:00 a.m. Maybe he would get some breakfast at the diner. He stared at himself in the mirror and slammed his hand against the sink. *No leads. Nothing. No leads on Toby or his cousin.*

Jack sighed and returned to his office. It looked like it would be another long day. Jack reached for his phone when he noticed Sandy standing in the doorway, holding two coffee cups in her hands.

Sandy blushed. "I spoke to Rafe yesterday, and he told me about Toby and Wynter. The office is closed today. I saw you in here and thought you could use one of these," she said as she extended a coffee to Jack.

Jack walked over to her and accepted the coffee. His eyes heated as he looked her over. She looked lovely with her fiery hair pulled into a ponytail. A few tendrils of hair framed her face. She was dressed in tight jeans and tank top with a blue-checked flannel shirt acting as a jacket. Jack took a sip of his coffee and sighed appreciatively.

"Thanks. I really needed this. You sure are a sight for sore eyes," Jack said with a smile.

Sandy returned the smile. "I'm glad there was something I could do for you. I know you've been working all night. Any news?"

Jack shook his head. "Not yet. I'm still waiting for results from our computer tech. Shit, this is just a mess. The FBI is working on finding Toby while we're trying to find Wynter."

"Is there anything I can do to help?" Sandy asked.

"You've already helped. I really appreciate you bringing me coffee."

Jack and Sandy stared at each other. The silence between them became a little uncomfortable. Jack cleared his throat. "I had a wonderful time on Saturday." Jack coughed. "Maybe, uh, we can get together again, you know, after we, umm, find Wynter and Toby?"

Sandy blushed again, the curse of redheads. "Yes, I would like that Jack," she whispered.

Jack's phone rang, startling them both. Jack looked at the phone and then back at Sandy. "I got to take that."

Sandy smiled. "I know. Go get your day started. I'll check in with you later."

"That would be great." Smiling, Jack reached for the phone as Sandy closed the door to his office. "Johnson here. Yeah, Dave, what ya got?" Jack frowned. "All right. Keep trying. If we can figure out where those payments in Thorpe's account came from, we might be able to find the guy behind these kidnappings. Call me when you get something." Jack hung up the phone and walked to the window.

If only something would break in the case, he thought.

※

Rafe clenched his hands into fists. Wynter was his dream girl. There had to be a way to connect without actually going to sleep. They were connected and shared a bond. All he had to do was access that bond. He rolled to his side and punched his pillow. All he needed to do was relax and concentrate. He put the fluffed pillow under his head and focused on his breathing. Slowly he breathed in. Then he slowly released his breath. He started with his feet, relaxing the muscles and then continued up, relaxing his legs. He continued his slow breaths relaxing his body until he was totally relaxed.

Rafe slipped into a meditative state and connected with Wynter. "Wynter, I knew we had a deep connection. I need to know if you are okay."

Wynter found herself on the swing in her backyard. "What are we doing here?"

Rafe wrapped his arms around her. "Sweetheart, tell me where you are. I don't know how long I can hold the connection."

Wynter sank into Rafe's embrace. "I'm okay. It's Toby I'm concerned about. One of the kidnappers keeps tormenting him. I'm afraid he'll hurt him before we're found."

"Can you tell me where you are?" Rafe asked.

Wynter frowned. "We're in a basement of a house."

Rafe stroked Wynter's hair. "Good. That's good, but do you know whose house you are in?"

Wynter looked inward, trying to get a lock on where she was. "I don't know if I can do this. I've never tried before."

"I know you can do it, Wynter. Try to relax and focus."

Wynter closed her eyes, trying to see where she was. She let out a cry of frustration. "I can't do it."

Rafe placed his hands on her cheeks. He looked deeply into her eyes. "You're a finder, so find the house where Toby is. You can do it."

Wynter closed her eyes and focused on Toby. Suddenly a picture formed within her mind. She opened her eyes and looked at Rafe. "The Mullen's place, just outside of town. Tell Jack. He'll know where we are. Hurry, Rafe. I'm so scared, and I think Toby is in real trouble."

Rafe pressed his lips to Wynter's forehead. "Hold on, darling. Help is on the way."

Rafe sat up and felt dazed. He did it. He connected

with Wynter. He jumped out of bed and went in search of his grandfather. Finally he found him in the kitchen.

"It worked, Grandfather. It worked. I was able to connect with Wynter. I know where she is. I gotta call Jack." Rafe fumbled with his cell phone and punched in Jack's number.

"Jack, I found her. She's at the Mullen's house. She said you would know where that is. I can't believe it. I connected with her. Tell me how to get there, Jack, and I will meet you. What?"

Rafe ran a hand through his hair. "Don't hand me that bullshit. I need to be there for Wynter. It's important, Jack. If you don't tell me, I'll just find out from someone else. Okay, okay, I got it. Thanks, Jack. I'll meet you there."

※

The big man got out of his car. He was wearing a blond wig. He had inserts in the sides of his mouth to change the shape of his face. He put on sunglasses to hide his eyes. *Good place to keep a hostage, a little farmhouse outside of town with no close neighbors. Too bad they couldn't follow orders*, he thought as he silently entered the house and headed for the basement.

As he walked down the basement stairs, he noticed that Wynter was tied to a chair, and she was screaming at Pete, whose pants were down around his ankles, cursing as he struggled to take the jeans off Toby. Toby wiggled, trying to get away, and screamed for help as he fought to get away from Pete.

Stupid bastard, always sampling the merchandise. Another fuckup on Oscar's part, hiring a perv, the big man thought. *Joey, the stupid fuck, was laughing. Too bad. The kid would have brought in a pretty penny. Another botched job. Look at those two idiots. They don't even know I'm here.*

"Excuse me, boys. There's been a slight change in plans."

Joey looked at the big man.

"What the fuck you doin' here?" Pete stood up and looked at the big man as he tried to pull up his jeans.

"The boss doesn't like the way you've been takin' care of business." The big man raised his gun and shot Pete in the balls. "That's for damaging the merchandise."

Pete screamed, clutching his crotch. Then he shot Pete between the eyes. The big man turned toward Joey.

"You forgot who you worked for, Joey. Now you gotta pay the price."

Joey held up a hand. "Wait …" he said as the big man shot him between the eyes. The big man looked around the room that had suddenly gone quiet. He stooped down and picked up his shell casings. He turned to Wynter and smiled a chilling grin.

"Today's your lucky day, lady," he said as he turned away to walk back up the basement stairs.

"Wait," Wynter said as she struggled with the zip ties. "You can't just leave us here."

Laughter echoed back down the stairs, and then she could hear a door being shut.

As the big man walked back to his car, he made a phone call to the boss. "Yeah, it's done. Ms. Malone is safe."

He heard sirens as he pulled his car out of the driveway. *Just in the nick of time*, he thought.

※

Wynter, her throat raw from screaming, wobbled on the chair, trying to get the attention of Toby, who was curled up in the corner crying.

"Toby," she croaked. "It'll be okay. Toby sweetie, please. Help is on the way. Just hang in there, kiddo," Wynter whispered as she watched Toby cry.

What the hell just happened? she thought, thankful they were still alive.

Wynter struggled with the ties, trying to get free from the chair and get to Toby, who was curled into a little ball on the mattress across from her. She wanted to scream out her frustration, but her voice was gone. *When will help arrive?* She couldn't get through to Toby. *God, I feel useless!*

"Toby …" she croaked.

Blood ran down her ankles and wrists. She opened her mouth to tell Toby that help was on the way, but no sound came out. Wynter froze when she heard footsteps on the stairs. *God, let that be help. Please, please, please let that be help.* Her heart stuttered. *What if it were that big man? Maybe he's coming back to kill us or, worse, finish what that perv had started with Toby.* She held her breath. She looked at Toby, who was still curled into a tight ball. A light flashed in her eyes. Terrified, she froze. She squinted, trying to see who held the flashlight.

Jack came into view with his gun drawn. Wynter

tried to call out to him, but her voice was gone. Jack saw Wynter in the corner, straining against her ties.

His breath caught when he saw Wynter tied to a chair. He looked beyond Wynter and saw a body lying on the floor. He walked over to the body and knelt down to check for a pulse.

Not finding one, he stood up, walked back to Wynter, and kneeled in front of her. "Oh, my God! Wynter, are you hurt? Where's Toby?"

Wynter stared mutely at Jack and then looked at Toby.

Jack turned his flashlight and walked over to the corner where Toby was curled into a ball. At the end of the mattress that Toby was curled up on was another body. Jack kneeled down to check if he were alive. Finding no pulse, he walked over to Toby and crouched down beside him.

Gently, he reached out and put his hand on his shoulder. "Toby, I'm Sheriff Johnson. You're safe, son."

Toby slowly looked up at Jack. "Are … are you Wynter's cousin?"

Jack smiled. "Yes, I'm Wynter's cousin, and I'm here to take you back to your parents." Jack reached over and scooped Toby into his arms. "It's okay. You're safe now. You'll be with your parents real soon, buddy."

Toby gripped Jack around the neck. "I wanna go home," he cried.

"I know, buddy. I know. We'll get you there soon." Jack walked to the bottom of the stairs. "Denise, down here. Wynter and Toby are down here."

Denise came down the stairs. She had pulled her blonde hair into a ponytail. She held her flashlight, and when she found Wynter, she ran over to her. She took her knife from its sheath and cut the zip ties that bound Wynter's wrists and ankles.

"Careful, Wynter. Those ties were very tight. Stay seated while I call for an ambulance." Denise said into her shoulder mic, "Dispatch, Deputy Blake here. We need an ambulance over here at the Mullen's old farmhouse ASAP. Affirmative. Send out Joe and his team. Over." Denise looked at Jack, who held a sobbing Toby. "Ambulance is on its way. Joe and his team should be here shortly."

Jack nodded and continued to rub Toby on the back.

Rafe came in behind Denise and ran over to Wynter. He gathered Wynter into his arms. "You okay, sweetheart? Oh God! Thank God. I love you, baby." Rafe gently wiped away the tears from Wynter's face. "I got you, honey." Rafe looked down at Wynter's wrists and tore his shirt to wrap around her wrists in order to stop the bleeding. "Christ, Jack! When is the ambulance going to get here? Wynter's bleeding."

Jack crouched down beside Wynter with Toby still in his arms. "God, Wynter. Rafe, wrap her wrists tighter. The ambulance should be here soon."

❋

Wynter and Rafe sat across from Jack, Sara, and Derek Steele in the conference room at the sheriff's office. Wynter had bandages on her wrists and ankles. Her larynx was damaged, and she was told not to speak, but still her statement needed to be taken. She wrote out what happened, and Jack, Sara, and Steele were looking it over. Rafe squeezed her hand. His voice was in her mind.

"I'm here with you." She would never forget Rafe's face as he stormed into the basement. He hadn't left her side, not for one minute, refusing to leave her at the hospital while the doctors examined her. She peeked up at Rafe and gave him a smile.

Steele tapped the picture on the table. "So this is the man that shot Joey Delgado and Pete Burns?"

Wynter nodded yes.

"He didn't make any attempt to hide his face from you?"

Wynter shook her head no.

Steele sighed. "We've run this face through several facial recognition programs, and we've got no hits. Do you know why this guy shot the other two?"

Wynter shook her head and pointed to her statement.

"Yeah, I read the report. So you think this guy was some type of cleaner. That Joey and Pete got messy and needed to be eliminated."

Rafe sat forward. "Yes, that's what she said in her report, Steele. Is this really necessary? The doctor told Wynter that she can't talk without doing some serious damage to her larynx. She wrote out everything she remembered. If there is nothing else, I'm taking Wynter home so she can rest." Rafe got up and pulled Wynter up with him. He glared at Steele and then nodded at Jack and Sara as he propelled Wynter out of the conference room. Steele watched the couple leave and sighed.

Jack drove up to Rosie Thorpe's house and sat in his car. *God, I hate bringing people news like this*, he thought. Slowly he got out of the car, walked up to the door, and knocked. Joe answered the door.

Joe took one look at Jack and flinched. "Come in, boss. Rosie's in the kitchen. I'll get her."

Rosie walked over to Jack. She kept pulling her sweater sleeves over her hands. "Hi, Jack."

"Hey, Rosie." Jack ran his fingers through his hair. "Rosie, Roger was"—Jack cleared his throat—"Roger was part of the kidnappings. We have proof that he received two large payments from Oscar Stanley, one of the kidnappers. His death is connected. We think that the head of this kidnapping ring was tying up loose ends …"

Rosie's breath hitched. "So that's how he was able to pay for the fertility treatments. Oh God, Jack! What do I say to Gabby or Mrs. Matthews? I had no idea …" Her hand went to her stomach.

Jack took Rosie's other hand in his. "Rosie, none of this was your fault. Roger made some bad choices, but none of this is your fault. Do you understand?"

Rosie nodded and turned to her brother, who gathered her in his arms. He looked over at Jack over her head. "Don't worry, Jack. I'll take care of Rosie. I appreciate you coming to the house to tell us. I'll talk to you later."

※

Jack was sitting behind his desk, staring blindly at the file on his desk, when Steele and Sara came in. Jack stood up.

"Hey, Sara, Steele," Jack said.

"Johnson, just stopping by to get a copy of your file in the Matthews case before we head back to DC," Steele said.

"I've got it right here," Jack said as he handed it to Steele. He looked at Steele. "Rafe's right. Wynter wrote out everything she knew. We know the big man is some kind of cleaner. So he is definitely not the boss. You now have a picture of one of the men behind this trafficking ring. We found Wynter and Toby before those men could do any serious damage. You have the names of the kidnappers, which should give you some leads to work with."

Jack looked at Sara. "I think you and Sara will find the bastard behind this."

Steele looked at Jack and shook his head. "We'll see."

※

Rafe and Wynter settled into the couch at Wynter's house. Rufus was snuggled next to Wynter on one side of the couch, and Rafe held her in his arms on the other side.

"God, I was so scared." Rafe looked down at Wynter as she rubbed his hand against her cheek. "I know I hurt you, Wynter. I freaked when I realized I could dream-walk in your visions."

Wynter put her finger against Rafe's lips. "You've explained, Rafe. I had time to think while I was tied up in that basement, and I know that you and I belong together. I want to give us that chance."

Rafe put his finger against her lips. "No talking. Let me get you some Earl Grey with honey." Rafe kissed

Wynter and leaned his forehead against hers. "We have a second chance. I'm not saying it'll always be easy, but I love you, and I can't imagine living my life without you. Just know that I am not going anywhere."

Wynter shivered. "Rafe, I need …" She put her hand over his heart and looked deeply into his eyes. "I need you, Rafe. I can still feel … I can still feel that evil. I know you think I'm not ready because of my injuries, but I need you more. I need to feel clean."

Rafe ran his hand through her curls. "Baby, I don't want to hurt you. I couldn't bear it if I caused you more pain."

Wynter took Rafe's hand and placed it upon her breast. "Loving me could never hurt me, Rafe."

Rafe stood and gently gathered Wynter into his arms. He carried her up the stairs to her bedroom. Gently he laid her upon the bed. "You're so beautiful."

Wynter blushed. "You're beautiful yourself."

"Only you think so," he said with a smile

Slowly he peeled off her clothes. His breath caught as he took in her beauty. Quickly he shed his own clothes. Rafe slid in bed next to her, careful not to jar her tender wrists and ankles. "God, I can't believe I almost lost you."

Wynter sighed as she placed her hand over his heart. "We almost let love slip away from us. You are my heart and soul. I was so sure, so afraid that you wouldn't be able to accept my gift. And now it seems to have grown. I don't have foresight—well, not much anyway—but that vision we shared was a first for me. I find things after they are lost. I usually don't have premonitions when someone is going to be kidnapped or share visions."

Rafe put his finger against Wynter's lips. "Shhh. You're not the only one who has fears. Our bond terrified me. I swore I would never dream walk another person's dreams, and there I was, sharing the most erotic dreams with a mysterious woman who had the most bewitching blue eyes I had ever seen. I lied to myself, telling myself I wasn't dream walking because they were erotic dreams. And who knows? Maybe it wasn't dream walking, but it was close enough that, when I finally met you in person, I was terrified, but I couldn't fight the connection I felt for you."

Wynter pressed a kiss at the base of Rafe's throat. "What a pair. I'm sorry that you felt responsible for your father's death. I should have known you weren't rejecting me, but …"

"Baby, how could you know? I didn't tell you about my dream walking." Rafe rained kisses down her throat. Gently he nipped her neck. "You had your own bad experiences." Rafe ran his hand down her body. His hand stroked her moist heat.

Wynter shivered as he ran his tongue around the rim of her ear. "You are so beautiful," he breathed. "So warm and responsive."

Wynter ran her hand down his chest, reaching for …

"No, let me give you pleasure," Rafe murmured. "This time is for you."

Slowly he licked his way down, finding her slick heat. Gently he sipped her sweet and addicting nectar.

She arched into his touch, moaning low. "Rafe," she whispered, "you are undoing me. I don't know how much longer I can last."

Rafe burned with a raging desire. Her body was so responsive, as if it were made for his touch. Through their bond, he could feel her love and her desire, creating a fire deep within his body, his soul. He felt the moment of her release as she clenched his tongue within her. Tremors undulated through her body. Carefully he positioned himself at her sweet entrance, pushing in slowly.

"God, baby, you feel so good." Rafe slowly pumped his hips and then increased his speed as pleasure raced through his body.

Wynter shuddered as another orgasm ripped through her. Rafe strained against her as he emptied his seed within her.

Rafe shifted his body as he gathered her in his arms. "That was perfect. We belong together. Never have I felt for anyone the way I feel for you. When I thought I lost you, I knew a part of me had died."

Wynter caressed his cheek. "Rafe, you don't know. When I thought those kidnappers were going to kill me, all I could think about was how much I loved you and how much I regretted not telling you how I felt. When you connected with me, I felt so blessed, and I knew then that if I survived I would do anything to make things right between us. I know together we can conquer anything."

"I love you," Rafe whispered, knowing they had a wonderful future together.

Wynter gave Rafe a bright smile. She believed him. This tragedy brought them together even closer than she could have imagined. Wynter laid her head on his shoulder and sighed. *Aunt Helen was right. Dreams really do come true.*

※

Oscar walked into his office, wondering why Joey wasn't answering his phone calls. *Dumb fuck. It looks like I am gonna have to make a trip after all.* Oscar sat down behind his desk and froze when he saw the big man leaning against the opposite wall. *What's he doin' here?* he thought.

"A new assignment?" Oscar asked as he loosened his tie.

The big man smiled. "Naw, no new jobs for you. The boss is cleaning house and wants to set an example," he said as he pulled out a dart gun. "Sleep well, Oscar. You're gonna need it," the big man said as he pulled the trigger.

Oscar's eyes widened in shock. "What the fuck?" he mumbled as he slumped over onto his desk.

The big man smiled.

※

Oscar jerked awake as he felt a cold liquid splash in his face. He choked as the liquid burned its way down his throat. "What the …" Oscar gagged on the fumes.

The big man poked him with a stick. "Nap time is over, Oscar."

Oscar slowly realized he was naked. His waist was tied to a tree. His hands were also tied around the tree, forcing him to hug a big tree.

"No wonder I'm freezing my ass off," he croaked. "What the fuck is going on?"

The big man smiled as he put down the lighter fluid and pulled out a spike, hammer, and knife. "I'm glad you asked. You fucked up, Oscar. Allowing your crew to damage the merchandise and doing jobs without telling the boss. Do you know how much money you cost the boss?"

"What the fuck are you talking about?" Oscar looked around frantically and pulled on the rope tying him to tree.

"Fucking stupid—that's what you are. Your crew fucked the kids, ripping them apart, making them worthless, you asshole. And now … now you pay," the big man said as he stepped closer to Oscar. "You have a choice to make, Oscar," he said as he drove the spike into Oscar's cock, nailing him to the tree.

Oscar screamed and then gagged as each breath he took caused excruciating pain.

"Scream all you want, Oscar. There's no one here to hear you," the big man said and laughed.

The big man walked around the tree and cut the tie from around his wrists. "I'm gonna give you this knife, and then I'm gonna set you on fire. You can stand and burn or cut and die. Your choice." The big man handed Oscar the knife and then set him on fire.

The big man turned and walked away, leaving Oscar to make his choice.

Derek Steele plopped down in his chair, stunned as he hung up the phone. *Christ*, he thought, *who did something like that?* Steele looked at Sara, who sat across from his desk.

"That was news on Oscar Stanley, the boss of Delgado and Burns. He was found dead in the woods not too far from Black Falls." Steele shuddered. "Christ, he was staked to a tree by his penis and then set on fire. They said a knife was clutched in his hand and he was trying to … well, I'm at a loss." He dropped his head into his hands. "Who is this fucking guy? Who is behind these kidnappings? I mean, Jesus, he killed off his whole crew. And what he did to Stanley …" Steele shuddered again.

Sara stood and stretched. "Well, Burke says he's working on a new lead. Also, we do have the picture of the big man. It's only a matter of time before we catch this guy."

Steele frowned. "We've had no hits on the picture. He might have changed his appearance. I mean, it makes sense. These guys are smart, and now they've killed off their weak link. I really hope you're right, Johnson. These guys need to be stopped."

19

Three Months Later

RAFE SAT BACK WITH a sigh. He couldn't believe how much his life had changed. He looked around the dining room table, thinking how grateful he was. Iris was showing her parents her new drawing. Jack, Helen, and Stuart were in deep conversation with his grandfather. Sara and Wynter were in the kitchen, putting the finishing touches on dinner. He had moved in with Wynter shortly after the kidnapping, and now they were planning their wedding. Though Gabby still struggled with letting Iris out of her sight, she was doing better. She was back baking at the restaurant. She and John now had a steady date night and were stronger as a couple than they were before. Jack was a mystery to Rafe.

He was interested in his secretary, Sandy, but had yet to ask her out again.

Wynter and Sara came back in the dining room laughing. *God, I love her*, he thought. *Yes, dreams really do come true.*

Printed in the United States
By Bookmasters